MYSTERY OF THE CRATER

Brander, the security chief of the Syrtis Base on Mars, isolates the entire emplacement when two men die from an unknown, alien disease. No one can enter or leave the base. Dr. John Naysmith, newly arrived on Mars, leads the medical team desperately trying to discover a serum to combat the virus. If they can't contain the spread of the disease Brander must annihilate the base and everyone in it with nuclear bombs! Then another three men become infected . . .

JOHN GLASBY

MYSTERY OF THE CRATER

Complete and Unabridged

LINFORD
Leicester

First published in Great Britain

First Linford Edition
published 2010

Copyright © 1972 by John Glasby
All rights reserved

British Library CIP Data

Glasby, John S. (John Stephen)
Mystery of the crater. - -
(Linford mystery library)
1. Extraterrestrial bases- -Fiction. 2. Viruses
- -Fiction. 3. Mars (Planet)- -Fiction.
4. Science fiction. 5. Large type books.
I. Title II. Series
823.9'14–dc22

ISBN 978–1–44480–068–5

Published by
F. A. Thorpe (Publishing)
Anstey, Leicestershire

Set by Words & Graphics Ltd.
Anstey, Leicestershire
Printed and bound in Great Britain by
T. J. International Ltd., Padstow, Cornwall

This book is printed on acid-free paper

1

John Naysmith was twenty-seven years old when he left the Aristarchus Base on the Moon and travelled to Mars.

It was eighteen years since his parents had perished in the disastrous attempt to establish the first lunar colony. During that time exploration had advanced to the point where four lunar cities had been set up, six manned landings had been made on Mars and the first interplanetary colony was now in existence in the Syrtis Major region.

Naysmith was a tall, thin man with the look about him of a man who had lived too close to the laboratory bench. His eyes were continually narrowed, as if he were perpetually staring at things too small to be seen without an electron microscope. His face was all shadows and angles. But in his own way he was a genius.

He had graduated from the University

of Maryland with a top degree in space biology — a subject, which, although purely speculative at the time of his studies, was to assume major importance before he was many years older. His memory was excellent, virtually photographic, enabling him to catalogue numerous facts in his mind and pull them out at a moment's notice.

But perhaps his most outstanding characteristic was the sense of urgency he conveyed to everyone around him; the feeling that there were great things to be done and little time in which to do them. Unfortunately, this made him intolerant of fools and those who failed to see his point of view, making him something of a social outcast.

He had been offered this field trip to Mars right out of the blue. There had been some speculation concerning possible areas on the planet where life might exist. What form this life might take he couldn't visualise because all of the earlier expeditions had reported that Mars was a totally sterile world; a place where life had either failed to come into existence because of a hostile environment, or had yet to appear.

The flight from Aristarchus had taken the best part of eight weeks. Eight frustrating weeks for a man of Naysmith's disposition. But at last it was over and he was standing beside the circular viewport of the ship watching the planet swinging up towards him.

Mars was not quite as deep a red as he had imagined and already he could make out the craters and other darker, more irregular, markings with the brilliant white of the south polar cap showing clearly around the limb. To one side, a little north of the equator, a wide surface region was obscured by one of the yellow dust clouds that were a more or less permanent feature of the planet.

The area around the viewports was crowded. In the crush Naysmith caught a glimpse of Jordan, one of the foremost selenographers of his day. They had had a number of interesting discussions during the long trip. Of all the passengers, Jordan was the one man he felt he could converse with on the same intellectual level. For this reason he had been attracted towards the other.

'It looks quite an impressive sight,' Jordan said, coming over to stand beside him.

Naysmith nodded. 'More so than the Moon. I'd like to think there's life down there that is native to the planet. Trouble is, though, we can't be absolutely certain even if we find any microorganisms there. They could have been introduced by one of the earlier expeditions.'

'But there'll have been the most stringent precautions against any outside contamination like that, won't there?'

Naysmith rubbed his jaw. 'I'd like to think so. But when you've worked with bacteria as long as I have you realise that it's the most difficult thing in the world to completely sterilise both men and equipment. During the first manned landings on the Moon there were bacteria introduced on the lenses of one of the television cameras. What's more important is that they were still capable of growth and division when discovered some months later.'

4

Jordan looked surprised. 'You mean they can live under conditions of vacuum?'

'Exactly. They're probably the most resistant of all organisms. They thrive under the widest known set of physical conditions. Of course they can't survive the heat generated during re-entry of a space probe but a soft landing might be a different proposition.'

Jordan nodded and said, 'Then your job must be an impossible one. I mean — how can you differentiate between any organism that was inadvertently introduced by ourselves onto Mars and those that are indigenous to the planet?'

'That's the big problem.' As he spoke, Naysmith watched the huge globe of Mars now swinging beneath them as they entered a stable orbit.

'But you don't think it's impossible?'

Naysmith did not answer immediately. The feeling of vagueness that was inside him was an unfamiliar one. He was used to making immediate decisions. Then he said, 'Certainly it won't be easy. Maybe I'm being pessimistic about the whole

5

thing. Maybe there are no bacteria of any kind down there.'

Jordan too was silent for a moment, contemplating the scene outside. After a while he said quietly: 'Have you thought this problem of yours through to its logical conclusion?'

'Meaning?'

'Just that if you're wrong and there are organisms of some kind on Mars then, sooner or later, in spite of everything we can do to protect the people in the colony, there could be an epidemic. And it may be a type of disease that is completely alien. One against which we have no protection at all.'

Naysmith's lips twisted into a thin line as he gave a brief nod. That possibility had been considered by many scientists for years, beginning with the first manned lunar landings. Strict quarantine regulations had been enforced then. But when nothing had shown up in any tests these regulations had been abandoned. Government circles were now convinced that no virulent bacteria existed on the Moon,

But Mars?

That was still very much of an unknown quantity. You could feed all the information you had into a computer and let it chew away on it for weeks but it never came up with any definite conclusion.

Certainly the colony here had been in existence for more than two years and nothing alarming had occurred so far. There had been one small epidemic ten months after its foundation but this had been due to a simple influenza virus, readily controlled by modern drugs and although there had been four deaths, it had not been the dreaded Martian plague as had at first been feared.

It had been pointed out many years before that virulent organisms capable of producing bizarre diseases in Man could arise from two distinct sources on extraterrestrial planets. Naysmith went over the information in his mind.

Where there was an atmosphere of any kind, and particularly in the presence of oxygen and water, the existence of native organisms unlike any found on Earth was more of a probability than a possibility.

So far, results obtained from sample cultures of Martian soil and air had yielded a great deal of conflicting evidence. This was, indeed, one of the problems he had been sent to Mars to resolve. It was also a debatable point as to whether such alien organisms had the ability to infect Man.

The second source rested with organisms transported from Earth to another world. Provided these could flourish in an alien environment there was a good chance that, in a very short time (for the regenerative cycle of a typical bacterium was extremely short), these would mutate into a species unknown on Earth. Yet being derived from terrestrial organisms these would almost certainly infect human beings.

'All passengers proceed to Airlock Seven. All passengers proceed to Airlock Seven.'

'I guess we go the rest of the way by shuttle,' Jordan remarked casually. 'Probably they daren't risk atomics in the atmosphere.'

They fell in with the other passengers

milling in the outer corridor, past airlocks five and six that were evidently for baggage, to the main airlock where a small group had already gathered. They waited. The faint jar as the small shuttlecraft from the surface locked tight against the outer hull came two minutes later. There was a gentle hiss of air as pressures equalised. Then the airlock door slid aside on grooved runners. One after the other they made their way into the shuttle rocket that was oddly cramped by comparison with the interplanetary ship.

Naysmith settled himself in a seat and peered through the small window as Jordan crushed into the other seat. The polished hull of the vessel they had just left stood out against the utter midnight blackness of space. By craning his neck, he could just make out the looming disc of Mars. Some of the major features he recognised from the maps he had seen back on Aristarchus Base.

There was Lacus Solis, a brilliant craterous formation in a wide reddish plain and off in the distance, near the limb, Syrtis Major stood out like a huge, curving elephant's trunk. There was so much to see on that ruddy disc that he was still sweeping his gaze across it when the shuttle dropped away from the planetship and arrowed down into the thin atmosphere of Mars.

They hit the upper atmosphere at a narrow angle like a flat stone skimmed across a pond, circled the planet once during the descent and then the braking rockets came on with a shrill scream.

Twenty-five minutes after leaving the planetship they landed with scarcely a bump on a concrete field immediately beside the cluster of transparent domes that formed the Syrtis colony.

The distant sun beat down from a pale, cloudless sky as they embarked in the large tracked vehicle that was to take them on the last short journey into the colony. Outside there were well-defined tracks in the ochre dust where constant traffic between the colony and the spaceport had left a hard-packed trail in the loose, friable surface of Mars.

Naysmith studied the scene outside. He was wondering what might lie beyond the looming crater walls that dotted the horizon. There must have been numerous expeditions beyond the region of the Base, he thought; searching parties looking for any sign of life, checking on mineral deposits, bringing in samples of ore from the desert, cans of dry ice and water from the polar region far to the south.

Inevitably, he found his thoughts turning to the four thousand million year gulf that lay between the birth of Mars and the present day. Surely something ought to have happened in that tremendous period and yet, for all they knew, Mars was like the Moon, sterile and empty. Inwardly, he found that very hard to accept.

Life, once it came into being, could be extremely tenacious.

The grinding tracks of the vehicle lifted a cloud of ruddy dust that settled only slowly. Back on the Moon, such dust tended to drift back to the surface almost at once but here there was sufficient atmosphere to hold it suspended for quite a time.

Several hundred yards ahead the nearest dome lifted from the flat surface. As the land-craft trundled towards it a rectangular opening appeared in the dome's side. A number of very curious-looking vehicles stood inside, just discernible in the dimness. There were tall cranes and derricks for cargo handling, spherical trucks with bulbous snouts mounted on huge balloon tyres and others, much larger, fitted with flexible tracks for negotiating more mountainous and rocky terrain.

They passed inside. The huge airlock door closed noiselessly behind them. The overhead lights came on, actinically bright, revealing everything in a harsh glare.

'Please remain in your seats until the dome has been pressurized,' called the driver over his shoulder.

On the panel in front of him a red warning light changed to amber, held steady for several minutes and then flicked to green. The driver got up from his seat. He turned and grinned broadly at them.

'Welcome to Syrtis Base,' he said warmly. 'I hope you all had a pleasant trip from Luna.' He spoke with a trace of accent, one that Naysmith did not recognise. Eastern European probably, he decided finally.

There were several murmurs of assent from the passengers as they pushed themselves upright, finding their legs in the unaccustomed gravity of Mars.

As they shuffled towards the door the driver called sharply:

'Is Doctor Naysmith here?'

'I'm John Naysmith,' he said. He looked up sharply, surprised at the mention of his name.

'Ah, good. I'd like you to come with me, sir.'

'Very well.'

Naysmith followed the driver outside, wondering what it was all about. As far as he was aware, very few people on Mars knew of this field trip. They walked between the rows of vehicles to a door at the far side of the huge dome. There was a printed sign just beneath a steadily-glowing green light which said simply: SYRTIS BASE. SECURITY DIVISION.

Naysmith stepped through after the

driver and found himself in a narrow room lit by a single bulb near the ceiling. The driver closed the door behind him and pushed a button on the wall. Naysmith felt the floor sink swiftly beneath his feet.

The descent was rapid but ceased in less than half a minute. His companion opened the door once more and ushered him through.

He was in a modern, sparsely-furnished room with antiseptically-white walls, a long desk and several chairs. Three men were seated at the desk facing him. The driver gave Naysmith a brief, friendly nod, then stepped back, closing the door behind him. There was a faint hum as the elevator ascended to the surface.

'Please sit down, Doctor Naysmith,' said the man in the centre. He indicated one of the chairs facing him. 'My name is Brander. These are Charles Leveritt and Karl Schwartzwald. You might say that we represent the security in Syrtis Base.'

Naysmith lowered himself into a chair and looked from one man to another. Take three men at random, he thought, and it would have been difficult to pick three so totally different. Brander was a gaunt, cadaverous individual with an almost skeletal face in which only his piercing blue eyes seemed alive. Leveritt was portly, jovial-looking with a blue-veined nose and a red flush on his sagging jowls. Schwartzwald was in his late forties but he looked as if he had been an athlete in his younger days and still kept himself in shape by regular exercise.

Naysmith pulled himself together. There was something here he didn't understand, a purpose deeper than appeared on the surface. Until he found out what it was, he would have to watch himself carefully. He had seen suppressed tension too often in the past not to recognise it immediately in all three men.

Some of his puzzlement must have shown through on his face for Leveritt said quickly. 'Sorry we had to drag you away from the others just as soon as you arrived. But we have something of a crisis on our hands.'

'I'm afraid I don't understand.'

'You will, Doctor Naysmith,' put in

Schwartzwald, his tone deceptively mild. 'You will.'

Brander cleared his throat. His brows went up a little, deepening the lines of strain that furrowed his forehead, etching his cheeks with even darker channels of shadow.

'I don't suppose you were told anything of your real mission on Mars before you left Luna.'

'Real mission?' Naysmith repeated. 'I was under the impression my trip here is to explore the possibility of life forms existing on Mars. A purely academic programme.'

'I'm afraid it was necessary for you to believe that until you actually arrived. Unfortunately, if the real reason should leak out we'd have a full-scale panic on our hands. That's something we must avoid at all costs.'

'Just what is the real reason then?'

Without replying, Brander turned in his chair and touched a button on the desk to his right. There was a faint click. The harsh lights dimmed and a screen on the wall behind him lit up to show a picture of a man lying on what looked like a hospital bed. It was several seconds before Naysmith realised he was looking at a corpse.

'This man,' Brander said harshly, 'was a member of a small research team investigating the region around Lowell. That's a fair-sized crater formation some thirty kilometres north of here.'

'What happened to him?'

Brander ran one hand absently through his thinning hair. 'He seemed perfectly healthy when he returned to Base with the others. Certainly he gave no indication of anything out of the ordinary. The following day, however, he complained of an intense headache, just behind the eyes. Apparently, it persisted for about twenty minutes or so and then wore off. The medical people diagnosed some form of migraine and let it go at that.'

'We should have insisted on a full medical examination there and then.' Schwartzwald said. 'It's possible we may have learned something important.'

'It's too late now to worry about what we should have done,' snapped Brander, his tone harsh and tense. 'It's done and that's all there is to it. Maybe now that Doctor Naysmith is here we can get to the bottom of it.'

'You still haven't told me how he died,' Naysmith said quietly.

His earlier feeling that these men were not only tense, but afraid, had intensified.

Brander swung his glance back from Schwartzwald. 'The point is that, less than eight hours later, this man made his way up to the surface level, manually opened one of the airlocks and walked out of the dome.' He paused, then added thinly. 'And without a suit.'

Naysmith frowned. 'He must have been temporarily insane.'

'I'd sleep more easily if only it were as simple as that,' Leveritt muttered. He drummed a brief tattoo with his fingers on the desk.

'He died instantly, of course,' went on Brander, ignoring the interruption. 'No one can live for more than a few seconds in that atmosphere out there.'

'And why do you think he didn't suffer a brainstorm, a temporary fit of insanity.

Men do sometimes go mad for no reason at all in an alien environment such as this.'

'This is the reason,' said Brander. He depressed the button once more and kept his finger on it.

On the screen the image expanded until the waxen face filled the screen completely.

'Take a close look at his eyes.'

Naysmith half rose from his chair and peered closely at the screen. He saw at once what the other wanted him to see. The dead eyes were wide open. They stared sightlessly from the screen into his. There was no pupil visible at all. Only a blank, empty whiteness.

The feelings the sight roused in him acted like an astringent. He felt his thoughts tighten and pull half a dozen wandering ideas into some form of unity. There was a little shiver of nameless fear running along his spine as he sank back into the chair.

'Now do you see?' murmured Brander, his words falling into a muffling silence.

'Yes.' Naysmith's voice was a husky whisper.

'Something out there caused this man's death. How, we don't know. But we have to find out what it was and how to combat it before it happens again. And there isn't much time.'

2

Less than ninety minutes after arriving at Syrtis Base, John Naysmith was in the underground mortuary looking directly at the first victim of what had now been termed the Lowell Syndrome. With him were Brander and Sen Corval. Corval was the doctor who had examined the dead man on his return from the ill-fated expedition. All three men wore snug-fitting plastic suits equipped with their own air supply.

If the cause of death was due to some unknown organism Naysmith considered the suits a somewhat belated precaution against infection. Nevertheless, he had insisted on it, preferring to take as few chances as possible in these odd circumstances.

For several moments the men said nothing but stood staring down at the still features and the curiously frightening eyes that stared up at them as if defying them to discover the answer.

'I'm glad you're with us, Doctor Naysmith,' Corval said finally, He looked distinctly unhappy behind the transparent mask. 'Because this is something completely outside my experience.'

Brander said, 'What gets me is why he should have run out onto the surface like that. He must have known it meant instant death.'

Naysmith bent and pulled back the white sheet that covered the man. No sign of any external marks or injuries. The arms and legs were well muscled. Obviously he had been a man who had taken care of himself. He shook his head as if it would drive out the blur of uncertainty that was confusing him. All these minutes he had been standing here trying to adjust to the simpler aspects of this situation that had suddenly been thrust on him. They were important — it was true — but these represented just the tiniest segment of all that was now happening on the Base.

His confusion and inner restlessness derived from a number of facts. He had expected to arrive on Mars to become involved in fairly leisurely research without any time constraints. His previous experience on Earth and Luna had all been of this kind. But to suddenly have to make hurried decisions based upon very little data was the last thing he had anticipated.

If only he had had some warning of this before he had left Aristarchus he could have spent those long frustrating weeks on the planetship far more profitably. The morality of keeping all of this a secret from him was a little too deep for Naysmith but just thinking about the way he had been deliberately kept in the dark brought a surge of anger.

Just what did these people expect him to accomplish in the short time that was possibly available? He fought down the anger because what had happened could not be changed. That was behind him. Ahead of him was the mystery of what had caused this man's death and curious condition.

'If this is a disease in the accepted sense of the word,' said Corval, 'its mode of action is totally different from anything I've ever come across.'

'If it's an organism native to Mars, surely that's what we would expect,' replied Naysmith.

'But what kind of madness would make a man react as he did?' Brander put in.

Naysmith shrugged. 'I can think of a lot of possible answers. Maybe it induced a sensation of uncontrollable claustrophobia. Perhaps he realised he was dying and wanted to get it over with as quickly and painlessly as possible. There may even have been intense pain at the end.' He sighed audibly. 'Those are just a few reasons and one thing we have to do, if possible, is decide which one is the most plausible.'

'That isn't going to be easy. You can't question a dead man.'

'The first thing to do,' said Naysmith decisively, recognising that it was now up to him to make the decisions, 'is to carry out some preliminary tests. How well are you equipped here for microbiological work?'

'Still pretty primitive in that respect,

I'm afraid,' Corval said. 'At least we are compared with Earth or Luna. We can prepare cultures for you, of course. I can also arrange for electron micrographs, chemical analysis, mass spectrometry and one or two other refined physical techniques to be carried out by the various departments.'

'That'll do for a start. I'll draw a couple of blood samples and take some skin swabs. They may tell me something. I'd also like some experimental animals if there are any. It's essential to find out if this condition, if it is caused by some unknown pathogen, can be transmitted by contact.'

'How long do you reckon such an organism can survive once the host is dead?' Corval asked.

'I only wish I knew. All we have to go on is the behaviour of typical terrestrial organisms and if we try to extrapolate from that to what we've got here, we may find ourselves chasing after shadows.'

'So we've to begin all the way from square one.'

'Afraid so. If we're dealing with an alien

organism we must put all preconceived notions out of our heads and be prepared to meet the utterly unexpected.'

He picked up the long-needled hypodermic from the sterile metal tray, bent, and inserted it deeply into the fleshy part of the man's back. After death, the blood always tended to move into the lowest part of the body and the man on the slab had been dead long enough for this to have happened, even in the lower gravity of Mars. The gloves made it difficult to work quickly and he cursed his clumsiness as he slowly withdrew the blood sample.

Corval held out the sterile evacuated tube and Naysmith thrust the needle into the rubber septum and carefully injected the sample into it.

'I suppose I'd better take a sample of the spinal fluid while I'm about it.'

For five minutes there was utter silence in the room. Naysmith worked as quickly as possible, swabbing the exposed flesh and running the swabs over the surfaces of various culture media in the Petri dishes the other two men held out for him, placing them in the chrome-plated container as he finished with each one.

'There.'

He straightened up. 'I think that's all we can do for the present. It will be some hours before we can tell anything definite from those cultures.'

'And the body?' Brander jerked a gloved thumb towards the corpse. 'I'd like to arrange for him to be buried as soon as possible.'

'Not yet, I'm afraid. These tests may prove negative. Then I'll have to carry out an autopsy.'

'Very well. If you think it's absolutely necessary.'

'It is.'

'Then I'll make the necessary arrangements.' Brander's agreement was reluctant.

He's scared, thought Naysmith, watching the security chief closely, and he's trying desperately not to show it.

'What about the animals?' he asked. 'I'll need them to check on how contagious this might be.'

Corval made a vain attempt to rub his chin. 'We've only got Black Norways.

27

They're standard laboratory animals used in most of the labs.'

'A couple of them will do for a start. I'd have preferred a Rhesus as well but if there are none available, I'll just have to make do with the rats.'

Inwardly, Naysmith felt surprised they had even this strain of rat here on Mars. It had been evolved several decades earlier when it had become apparent that, if scientific tests were to be carried out in laboratories all over the Earth there had to be a strain of animal that was genetically uniform if such tests were to have any real meaning. The descendants of the true Black Norway were now small, white animals, extremely docile and well suited to the numerous tests that had often to be carried out.

When he came to consider it, of course, it was only logical that they should have a supply of these rats on Mars. The possibility of a completely new disease appearing on the planet had been in the minds of most scientists ever since the idea of setting up a colony on Mars had been seriously contemplated. On the

Moon it had not been necessary since they now knew, quite definitely, that there were no indigenous species of bacteria flourishing in that utterly sterile environment.

Corval went out taking the samples with him. When he had gone, Brander said softly; 'You think it is some form of disease peculiar to Mars, don't you?'

Naysmith thought: 'He desperately wants me to say no and yet he's already made up his mind what it is. And I'm not going to be rushed into anything, not at this stage.'

Aloud, he temporized: 'If you want a definite answer to that I'm afraid I can't give you one. Not at the moment, anyway. Certainly all of the evidence points in that direction. The only other possibility that suggests itself is some form of radiation sickness.'

The security man shook his head inside the plastic suit. 'We considered that at the outset. We've been over the vehicle and the other men on that expedition. Not a trace of radiation.'

'Then that eliminates that possibility.'

'Besides,' went on Brander, 'Mars seems to be extremely deficient in radioactive materials. We've had a number of teams out looking for such deposits but without any success. The heavier chemical elements seem to be missing from the Martian crust.'

'Cosmic radiation, perhaps?'

Behind the transparent mask, Brander pursed his lips into a thoughtful line. 'That's possible, I suppose. But why were the others not affected? We've had them all under constant observation in an isolation ward since this happened. They all seem healthy enough. And they're all demanding to be released. We can't keep them there forever.'

Naysmith hesitated, trying to figure out a rational explanation. Finally, he said, 'There could have been a defect in his suit. Even so, from what we know of cosmic radiation it doesn't produce anything resembling this.'

And the eyes, he thought. Whatever had happened to this poor devil had destroyed the pigment of the pupil. That was really the only significant fact he had to go on.

Brander moved across to the other side of the room. He had his hands clasped tightly behind his back and there was a worried frown creasing his thin face.

'There's one other point I have to raise, Naysmith. Sooner or later we'll have to release this information to Earth. If this thing should get out of hand we'll be forced to set up quarantine measures.'

'You've obviously kept it quiet so far.'

'Naturally I thought it best in the circumstances. They know we have a biological problem on our hands but I gave them only a few of the details, just sufficient to ensure they sent us someone with the necessary knowledge to fight it.'

'You've not told them how serious it really is?'

'Not really. At the moment there's just this one man. But if it is contagious, we might have a full-scale epidemic here. That would be disastrous. It might even wipe out the entire colony.'

It might indeed, reflected Naysmith. There had been pandemic plagues on Earth throughout the ages that had resulted in millions of deaths. Even there it had been possible for people to flee the plague by going to parts of the country where it had not struck. But the Martian colony was a closed system. There was nowhere anyone could go to get away from this and there was no chance of anyone being allowed off the planet to make for Earth or Luna. Such a course would be inviting mass suicide.

'How long do you reckon you can keep silent about the true facts?' he asked.

'Not long. A week or so at the most.'

Naysmith whistled faintly through his teeth. 'That doesn't give me much time.'

'I'm sorry.' Brander sounded as though he really meant it. 'You've got a really tough job on your hands. All I can promise you is every facility we have on the Base. Naturally, this has top priority. If you need any of our equipment or services, just ask and I'll see you get them right away.'

'Thanks. I'll do that.'

Corval came back into the mortuary at that moment. He carried a small cage in which were two of the rats.

Opening the tiny door, Naysmith

reached in and took one of them out, holding it gently in his gloved hand. He went across to the slab and placed the animal on the flesh of the naked corpse. The rat sniffed experimentally at the air. Then it commenced walking slowly over the unmoving chest. Naysmith allowed it to remain there for several minutes. Then he replaced it in the cage and repeated the procedure with its companion.

'I want these kept isolated and under constant observation,' he said finally. 'Do you have any trained technicians who can do that?'

Corval nodded. 'I'll see to it.'

'Make sure they understand all the precautions. And let me know the moment anything out of the ordinary happens. It doesn't matter how trivial it may seem.'

* * *

Half an hour later Naysmith sat in the small canteen eating his first meal since landing on Mars.

He had almost finished when someone

sat in the seat opposite and glancing up he saw it was Jordan. Placing his plate on the table, the selenographer said in a low voice: 'I've been looking all over for you. What was all that about at reception? The way they hauled you off I thought you might be an unwanted immigrant. I half expected you'd be pushed back to Luna on the next trip.'

Naysmith forced a faint grin. Jordan was the last person he had wanted to meet at that moment before he got his thoughts into some kind of order. Any other of the passengers he could have fobbed off with any sort of story. But Jordan was also a scientist and he wouldn't believe just anything.

'Nothing really important,' he said finally, forcing evenness into his voice.

'You can't fool me, John. I've known you for too long. There's something wrong here, isn't there? I've been hearing some whispers during the past couple of hours from various people.'

'What sort of whispers?' Naysmith countered.

'Something about a new sort of bug

brought back by one of the scientific expeditions. Was that the real reason they sent you here?'

'If they have discovered some new organism I'd certainly like to hear about it. It's true they are worried in case they have another outbreak of influenza like the last one. That's all.'

'Then why go to all the trouble of bringing you out from Luna? Can't their own medical folk handle it?'

Naysmith shrugged and pushed his empty plate away from him.

'I'm afraid you're missing the point. Most of the people here have been away from Earth for more than a decade. They came originally from Aristarchus Base. At least seventy children have been born since this colony was established so I reckon you can technically call them Martians. And that number will soon have doubled, trebled. Once this second generation come along they'll have lost most of the immunity to disease the folk back on Earth have. They'll be wide open to even the common cold if it's brought in by newcomers to Mars.'

Jordan chewed reflectively on a mouthful of vegetables. 'Like the Red Indians and the Australian aborigines, you mean?'

'Something like that,' Naysmith agreed.

'And they think you can do something about it?'

'I can try. Unfortunately there's still a lot we don't know in the field of immunology.'

'Then I wish you luck,' Jordan stirred his coffee, staring at Naysmith across the table. 'I'm glad my particular field is a little less complicated than yours.'

There was a moment of silence. Naysmith finished his own caffeine-free coffee and set the cup down in front of him. 'Tell me, do you know much of the make-up of the Martian surface?'

Jordan glanced up in surprise, his cup halfway to his mouth.

'Why this sudden interest in the surface of the planet? Are you planning on going out there?'

'Maybe. If I'm to discover whether any life exists on Mars, I'll have to go out and see things at first hand.'

'Funny. I hadn't thought of that. I'd always associated you with the medical profession, seeking cures for new and unknown diseases. I guess I forgot your main interest is searching for the bugs themselves. Any particular region of Mars you're interested in?'

'Eventually I hope to get in with one of the expeditions to the south polar region.'

Jordan finished his coffee. 'Well, there's little doubt it's the most likely place to find some form of life. They've detected water there as well as solid carbon dioxide and I guess you've read that paper by Stephens and Drayton in which they claim to have found evidence for amino acid formation in some of the shallower crater formations there.'

Naysmith nodded. Amino acids were the building blocks for proteins and, eventually, for life itself. Naturally, it was a big step from a protein molecule to a unicellular organism but it had happened on Earth and he saw no scientific reason why it shouldn't happen here.

The theory that life on Earth had originated in some primeval soup formed of large molecules suspended in water had been suggested around the middle of the past century. Experiments carried out in the United States in which electrical discharges were passed through gases simulating the original producing atmosphere of Earth had resulted in the production of numerous amino acids.

Then there was the theory put forward by Hoyle some time later that life had been carried to Earth in cometary debris. Even if that were true such a theory also applied to Mars.

Later experimenters Kalevsky and Durarkin had created simple cells complete with cellular walls and protoplasm by the synthesis of DNA and ribonucleic acids. Artificial organisms could thus be produced in the laboratory by a process strikingly analogous to the natural reproductive cycle. The precise details of their synthesis were extremely complex requiring the use of a massive computer system but there was no doubt that life, on this lowly level, had been created.

He grew aware that Jordan was speaking again. 'I've been checking with the geologists here and there's a region much closer than the pole where you might find something of interest.'

'Oh, where's that?'

'It's a smallish crater about thirty kilometres from here.'

'Lowell?' Naysmith's tone was sharper than he had intended.

'Why, yes.' Surprise showed momentarily on the other's face.

'You've heard of it?'

'A little. It's one of the areas I have on my list of possible sites to visit.'

'You're sure that's all there is to it? Lowell hasn't anything to do with that mysterious conference you had on arrival?'

'Of course not. And as I've said, there was nothing mysterious about it.'

Jordan's expression said plainly that he did not believe him, but the selenographer did not question him further. He finished his coffee, drinking it noisily. Then he wiped his mouth and scraped back his chair.

'I'll try to get you some more information on Lowell. It's possible I can arrange a visit out there in the near future. If you're still interested, maybe you'd care to come along.'

'Of course.'

Jordan left and Naysmith sat where he was for several minutes trying to sort things out in his mind. The idea of visiting Lowell had been at the back of his mind for some time but it had been pushed out of the way by more immediate problems. Everything had happened too swiftly.

The possibility that there was something strange associated with the region around Lowell could not be dismissed or ignored. But at the moment he couldn't even hazard a guess at what it might be. New planets had a habit of springing unpleasant surprises but this just didn't make any sense.

Was it an extremely localised phenomenon? How long had it been in existence? If it was the seat of some alien infection, why hadn't it spread over more of the surface due to the atmosphere and the ever-present dust storms? Where? How? Why? He caught his whirling mind, drew it in and brought it into focus. The most important fact was — what kind of organism were they dealing with?

He got up. It was time to go along to the Pathology Department and check on those samples and see how the rats were faring.

With the new pressures of time that Brander had forced upon him, the results of the tests had suddenly assumed a great importance. Naysmith hoped that with their shorter lifespan, the rats would soon show symptoms similar to those the dead man had undergone before he had dashed inexplicably out onto the Martian surface without a protective suit. In addition, the culture plates ought to show some indication of living organisms and among them it might just be possible to locate that which had caused this man's death.

It was thus with a feeling of excitement that he made his way along the white, antiseptic-smelling corridor towards a door at the far end marked:

PATHOLOGY DEPARTMENT
AUTHORIZED PERSONNEL ONLY

He knocked loudly on the glass panel. There was a pause and then the door was opened by a girl dressed in a white coverall.

'Yes?' she said. Carefully pencilled eyebrows went up in interrogation.

'I'm John Naysmith,' he said, introducing himself. 'I — '

'Oh yes, of course. Please come inside, Professor Naysmith.'

'It's just Doctor Naysmith,' he corrected, permitting himself a faint smile. He went inside and she closed the door behind him.

The laboratory was smaller than he had expected. The equipment set out on the benches however looked modern and sophisticated. Two other technicians were busy at work in one corner, examining slides under viewing microscopes. There was a computer link standing on one bench with a video screen in front of it. And against the far wall he saw the gleaming bulk of an electron microscope. As he stared at it in surprise, the girl said: 'I'm Carine Wilder. I see you're admiring our latest acquisition. Actually, we had it brought down here an hour ago on Doctor Corval's instructions. He thought you may want to use it.'

'That was very thoughtful of him.' Naysmith had not used an electron microscope for a couple of years and his knowledge of the advances made was, perhaps, a little behind the times.

'We're linked in to the main computer on the Base,' the girl explained. 'If you need any calculations carried out they're almost instantaneous. For most of the time it's not in continuous use.'

Naysmith nodded his head. 'That's fine. Right now I'm more interested in the samples I sent in and also the two Black Norways.'

'I'll get them right away.'

She went over to a pair of ovens, thermostatted to remain within a hundredth of a degree of the temperature setting. Bringing out the Petri dishes she laid them on the polished bench near one of the viewing microscopes. As he bent over them, scanning the smooth surface of the nutrient agar, Naysmith realised, quite suddenly, that none of them were wearing protective clothing.

'There's nothing there at all,' Carine

said quietly. She glanced up at him. 'Is this what you expected?'

He shook his head decisively. 'Definitely not. But it's what I feared.'

'I'm afraid I don't understand.'

'Can we examine these dishes under the microscope?'

'Oh, yes. The stages are equipped to handle dishes this size quite easily.' She picked up the nearer Petri dish and slid it onto the microscope stage. After she had adjusted the focus and arranged the instrument for viewing by incident light, she stepped back a couple of paces.

On the wide rectangular viewer above the eyepiece, the surface of the agar seemed perfectly smooth and featureless.

'I'll set it up for automatic scan,' Carine touched a small knob and immediately the stage commenced to move slowly from right to left. 'It will continue scanning the whole surface for as long as you wish,' she explained softly.

For almost an hour, the scanning continued. First they examined the smear from the blood sample and then that of the spinal fluid. In both cases there was nothing to be seen, nothing that bore any resemblance to a bacterial or fungal colony growing on the nutrients.

'What do you make of it?' he asked finally, straightening up.

'I don't know.' Carine furrowed her brow in perplexity. 'I'd have expected something to show. I mean the normal terrestrial organisms present in the blood, at least. But absolutely nothing . . . '

Naysmith sighed. 'Let's take a look at the rats. I doubt if we'll learn anything more from these plates.'

Thus it was that Naysmith made his first serious error, one that he did not recognise for two full days afterwards. He failed to recognise that there were at least two possible reasons why the plates should have been sterile.

In the wire-mesh cage the two rats were still alive and showing no ill-effects. In a way, thought Naysmith, this was predictable from the negative results obtained in their microscopic examination of the culture plates. If they were sterile, it was only logical that the rats could not have contracted any infection.

He stared down at the two animals as they scampered happily around the floor of the cage. 'They seem quite normal. But we'd better keep them under observation. At the moment, in spite of the evidence from the cultures, we have only a rudimentary idea of the induction period of this disease.'

'Then you are sure it was caused by some pathogen?'

'Right now, I'm not sure of anything. Maybe I'm just used to thinking like a microbiologist. If it isn't, then we're wasting our time. But until we find any evidence to the contrary, I think we ought to proceed on the assumption we're dealing with some kind of pathogenic organism.'

'And in spite of these preliminary experiments it may still prove to be contagious?'

'That's always a strong possibility in a case like this,' he said soberly.

3

Directive SB 17-5Z was a built-in safety measure which had been available to the Security Department of the Syrtis Base ever since it had been established. In essence, it provided a means of completely isolating the base in the event of a biological crisis and called for the recall of all exploration teams, their complete quarantine on return, and the cessation of all space flights between Mars and Earth or Luna.

The decision to put the directive into effect was made two days after Naysmith arrived at the base. It was precipitated by two events that occurred within hours of each other.

John Naysmith learned of these while in the Pathology laboratory working on the two rats that had been exposed to the corpse in the mortuary.

Much of his work had settled already into a routine, a strangely mechanical rhythm in which the hour of the day or night did not seem to count in the overall scheme of things. So far, most of his experiments had led him nowhere. At first, this had not proved too disappointing. He had expected it. As a research scientist he was well aware that probing like this into unknown fields meant treading many and varied paths which led away from the eventual solution of the problem.

Very often, as he knew from past experience, it was not sheer hard work nor intuition that paid dividends in the end. Rather it was the lucky break that might come when least anticipated. As yet, however, this hoped-for break had not materialised.

Now he bent, examining the rats as they ran around the floor of the cage. Carine Wilder stood at his elbow, watching intently.

'Still nothing,' he said finally. He straightened up with a sigh. 'I don't understand it. If they are contaminated with the organism I would have expected something to have shown up long before this. Their metabolic rate is far higher than that of a human being.'

'Unless they really are immune to this disease.'

It's strange, Naysmith thought, but already we've got into the habit of accepting that it is some disease caused by a natural pathogen of Mars. But we've absolutely no proof even of that. We still know nothing for certain.

'I keep wondering about natural immunity,' he said after a pause. 'We'd better take another look at that corpse. I think the time has come to carry out an autopsy.'

'I'll put in a call for Doctor Corval. I'm sure he'd like to be there to assist.'

Naysmith nodded. Carine Wilder was halfway across the room when the buzzer on the desk shrilled loudly. She turned quickly, went over, and lifted the receiver.

'Yes, he's here,' she said after a moment. She held the receiver out to him.

Naysmith had an uneasy feeling as he took it from her. 'Doctor Naysmith speaking.'

'Doctor. This is Brander. I want you in my office right away. Drop everything you're doing. This is urgent.'

'I'll be there in five minutes, I'd like to bring my assistant with me if I may.'

'Who's that?'

'Carine Wilder. Pathology Lab.'

He glanced across at the girl as he spoke. There was a slight pause at the other end of the line. Naysmith could visualise Brander searching through the computer that was his mind until he located the name and decided whether or not she represented a security risk.

'All right. Bring her along.'

There was a click and the line went dead as the other broke the connection.

'What is it?' Carine asked as he replaced the receiver. She watched him keenly.

'I'm not sure. Brander didn't say anything over the phone. But it's trouble, I think. We're to report to his office at once. Something important must have come up.'

'Something to do with this problem?'

'Must be. I can't think of anything else

that would make him drag us away from here. We'd best get down there right away.'

Hanging his white coat on the peg beside the door, he threw on his jacket. He felt inwardly annoyed. If Brander expected him to have any answers ready he was going to be disappointed. This problem was not going to be solved as quickly as that. He could understand the security chiefs worry but he doubted if Brander understood any of the difficulties they were facing.

As he made his way along the curving corridor with Carine beside him, Naysmith found himself involuntarily considering all of the possibilities for this call. Overwhelming among them was the likelihood of another case being reported or that some communication had been received from Luna.

As they came within sight of Brander's office, Corval came hurrying along from the opposite direction.

'Have you been summoned too?' He looked more worried than usual, deep lines ploughed across his receding forehead. 'You any idea what it's all about?'

Naysmith shook his head. 'No more than you do,' he said. 'No doubt Brander will soon enlighten us.' His attempt at flippancy was only half-hearted.

Rapping on the glass panel, Corval thrust the door open, stood on one side to allow Carine to precede him, then ushered Naysmith inside.

'Sit down, please.' Brander indicated the chairs set out facing him. 'Sorry I had to drag you away like this but we have a second crisis on our hands.'

'Another like the first?' Naysmith asked.

'Afraid so.' Brander gave a terse nod, the lines of worry deepening. He pulled a small receiver towards him.

'This is a recording of a message that came through from one of the surface teams less than fifteen minutes ago. I want you all to listen to it carefully.'

He pressed the button. There was a soft burr, followed by a crackle of static that lasted for perhaps ten seconds, then a faint voice was superimposed upon the background noise. Deftly, Brander turned the volume up as far as it would go. The voice sounded high-pitched and taut as though the owner were having some difficulty in speaking coherently.

' . . . from Rover Seven. Syrtis Base from Rover Seven. Do you read me? Over.'

A slight pause, then: 'For Christ's sake, why don't you answer? Calling Syrtis Base. Calling Syrtis Base. Over.'

Another voice broke in at that moment. A calm and reassuring voice.

'Telfer. Communications Officer at the base,' Brander said.

'This is Syrtis Base, Rover Seven. Go ahead. Over.'

'Thank God. I thought we'd never get through. Listen. Something has happened here that we don't understand. Gordon is dead. He must have deliberately taken off his suit without any of us noticing. Then he simply opened the rear exit of the crawler and jumped out onto the surface. We stopped and pulled him back on board but he died almost instantly. Over.'

There was a moment of howling static that drowned out everything else. Naysmith felt his ears protest. Then the sound faded and Brander's voice came from the recording.

'Rover Seven. This is Major Brander. Pull yourself together, man, and listen very carefully. This is vitally important. According to your programme you were to investigate the area around Lacus Solis. Are you returning directly to base and have you made any unauthorised diversions at all from your scheduled route? Over.'

'We made one diversion, Major. Gordon wanted to take a look around Lowell on the way back. Over.'

Lowell again!

Naysmith felt a little shiver pass through him as he sat tautly upright in his chair. There had to be something there. This was stretching coincidence a little too far. Once again he felt his mind on the verge of asking a hundred burning questions but he forced himself to concentrate on the recording.

'I see.' Brander's voice again. 'And did Gordon complain of any fever or other symptoms after you left Lowell? Over.'

A longer pause, then: 'He did say

something about having a headache yesterday around noon. But it soon passed off and he seemed okay. Why — is this important? Over.'

'I'm afraid it may be. I want you to head for Base immediately. Once you arrive, you'll all go into quarantine. This is a purely precautionary measure but a very necessary one in the circumstances. Do you understand? Over.'

The hiss of intruding static reached a momentary crescendo. Then it subsided so that only part of the other's reply could be heard.

' . . . will arrive in twenty-five minutes at maximum speed. Over and out.'

The recording hissed and then fell silent as Brander depressed another key. He lifted his head slowly and stared at them across the desk.

'They should be here within the next ten minutes or so. I've made all of the necessary arrangements for ensuring they're completely isolated once they arrive. Not only the men, but also the crawler. Now there's only a little time in which to consider our next step.'

Naysmith ran his tongue over lips that were suddenly dry. He cleared his throat, then said: 'Exactly the same symptoms as the other case. And once again, that region around Lowell comes into the picture. I assume that until all this started, you had expeditions going out to various areas of Mars and all without incident.'

'That's true. The expedition of nine weeks ago was the first to Lowell.'

'Then we must go on the premise that, whatever it is, it's strictly localised.'

'So how does that fit in with it being some form of alien microorganism? Surely it would spread, and quite rapidly too, due to wind and dust storms.'

'That's what has been nagging at me ever since the possibility was put forward. At the moment, I can see no mechanism that would keep bacteria or a fungus in one small region of the planetary surface. On the Moon, perhaps. It may be possible there. But not on Mars.'

'Then where does that get us?' put in Corval. He sounded tired, and frustrated.

'I'm not sure. Perhaps nowhere. But if

we could only find the answer to that question it might go a long way towards solving several others.'

'Presumably,' Corval said. He glanced round at Brander. 'Do you honestly think you can keep these men in isolation for long? If this disease is contagious it will mean we have to keep them in quarantine until we find an antidote or until they die.'

Brander spread his hands in a gesture of futility. 'I've got no other choice.'

'Can you ensure there's no possible way out of the isolation quarters?' asked Carine, leaning forward.

'I think so,' Brander drew his brows down into a bar-straight line. 'Why do you ask?'

'I should have thought it obvious. Two men have died in mysterious circumstances, both by getting out onto the surface without any protective clothing. Clearly something must have driven them to it. Either it was some form of insanity or — '

'Or they were trying to escape from something,' finished Naysmith. There was a trace of undisguised excitement in his voice. 'Why didn't we think of that, before?'

Corval looked puzzled. 'It doesn't make sense. They were both quite safe and secure. One man in the dome and the other in the crawler. What could they possibly have been trying to get away from? And why take off their suits first knowing they were the only things which could keep them alive?'

'I can't answer your last point because I agree that at the moment it doesn't make any sense. But I can see what Carine's getting at. If we make certain they can't get out we can observe their reactions and possibly communicate with them. You'd better set up a two-way communicator in that quarantine area.'

'Shouldn't be any difficulty about that,' acknowledged the security chief, nodding. 'Clearly they must be kept under strict observation all the time. But can this thing be contagious after all? Those men in the other expedition wandered all over the base before we realised there was anything wrong. Surely there would have been other cases before now if it can be transmitted from one person to another.'

'Maybe we just had a lucky break,' suggested Corval.

Naysmith sat back in his chair. He frowned. Somewhere, at the back of his mind, there was the feeling they had overlooked something, some little fact that was vitally important.

One fact alone kept hammering away at his mind. Both of these men had deliberately removed their suits before stepping out into the alien atmosphere of Mars. That took time and, presumably, deliberate thought. It was not as if something had happened within a split second, overriding all conscious actions. Certainly no man in his right mind would do such a thing. Some intense feeling of claustrophobia was an answer but somehow he didn't think it was the correct one. There was something else but no matter how hard he tried he couldn't think of any other alternative.

Brander rose wearily to his feet, pushing his chair back quickly. He stood for a moment resting his weight on his

59

hands, fingers flat on top of the desk. He said heavily: 'We'd better get ready for that crawler when it arrives. There can't be any mistakes this time.'

* * *

On the circular viewer Naysmith made out the squat, ugly shape of the approaching crawler.

It lifted a heavy cloud of reddish dust in its wake and the pale sunlight glinted off the thick metal and transparent observation shields. He estimated it was about a mile away but it was making good time. He figured that the crew were not relishing the prospect of spending an indeterminate time in quarantine but set against this they would not want to remain in the company of their dead companion any longer than was necessary.

The crawler came within two hundred yards of the nearest dome and then turned in a sharp circle as it made its way towards the small dome some distance from the main cluster of humped buildings.

A door slid open in the side of the dome and two minutes later the crawler vanished inside. The door closed and there was only the broad track in the sand to mark its recent passage.

Brander touched one of the controls. The picture flicked off and was replaced a second later by one of the interior of the quarantine building. The air pressure must have equalised for the crew were already clambering from the crawler and standing around uncertainly in a small group.

Flipping down the communicator switch, Brander said harshly: 'This is Major Brander. I want you all to listen carefully to what I have to say,'

On the viewer, Naysmith saw the men jerk up their heads, staring in the direction of the two-way communicator on the wall.

'This is an emergency. One man from the official expedition to Lowell has already died here in circumstances that suggest that he contracted a fatal disease due to some unknown organism. The symptoms were identical to those you

61

reported for your colleague. Until we can isolate and identify the microorganism responsible and devise some form of antidote I'm afraid you must all remain isolated from the rest of the Base.'

The men near the crawler turned to stare at each other and Naysmith could imagine the thoughts that were running through their minds at that moment. Almost certainly, the first thing they would think of was that this disease was both highly contagious and inevitably fatal. That the bug which had resulted in the strange death of Gordon was already coursing through their bloodstreams, spreading its insidious poison through their bodies.

A voice he recognised as that on the recording said hoarsely over the communicator: 'How long do you intend to keep us here, Major?'

'Only until we know what we're dealing with and how to destroy it.'

'But that could take weeks, months.' There was a rising hysteria in the man's tone now.

'We're working on the problem with all

possible speed. Believe me, the best men have been assigned to the problem, which has top priority. We feel certain we'll have it licked within a few days at most. In the meantime, try to make yourselves comfortable. Everything you need will be provided.'

'It's all very well to say that, Major. But if you think we're just going to sit here and wait to die, you're wrong.'

The man who had spoken suddenly turned and ran for the door leading into the intercommunicating tunnel. He reached it in seconds and twisted the handle, hauling on it savagely.

'All exits have been secured.' Brander went on, trying to keep all trace of emotion out of his voice. 'Just try to remain calm and do as we ask. We'll make far more rapid and positive progress that way.'

Gradually, sanity prevailed among the crawler crew. The one who had first spoken — Naysmith took him to be the leader of the expedition — drew in a deep breath and said; 'What do you want us to do, Major?'

'That's better. I want you to remove

Gordon's body from the crawler and place it on the conveyer belt along the wall. Once that's done, we'll remove it for examination. Then I'm afraid I shall have to ask you some further questions. It's imperative we know everything that happened around Lowell.'

In the quarantine dome, Gordon's body was taken from the rear of the crawler by two of the men and carried across to the conveyor. Once it had been laid on it the belt began to move slowly, carrying the inert body through a rectangular opening in the wall. When it had passed out of sight the wall section snapped back into place and Naysmith guessed that it was self-locking. There would be no way out by that route for any of the men who might try to follow.

Brander turned to Corval. 'There's your patient, doctor,' he said wearily. 'He'll be taken through to the isolation chamber in Pathology Department. I suggest that you handle him from outside and take all the precautions you can think of — and then some.'

As Naysmith made to follow Corval,

Brander went on: 'Do you wish to help Corval, Doctor Naysmith? Or are there any questions you'd like to ask these men concerning Lowell?'

Naysmith paused. There was no doubt that Corval and Carine could perform the autopsy without his help and there were certain things about Lowell that had been bugging him for some time. This seemed the ideal opportunity of trying to get some answers.

'Thanks. I guess I'll stay and hear what these men have to say. They may have noticed something important.'

'Then ask away.'

Naysmith took the security chief's place at the transmitter. The nearness and the clarity of the picture on the viewplate made it difficult to realise that these men were nearly a kilometre away from where he stood. He might almost have been standing on a balcony looking down at them.

'I'm Doctor Naysmith,' he said slowly. 'And I want to assure you men that as far as we know, you're in no danger. I'd like to ask you some questions about Lowell

65

and afterward, if there are any questions you'd like to ask me I'll do my best to answer them.'

'All right,' said the leader of the expedition. 'Go ahead, Doctor Naysmith. What is it you want to know?'

'Was Gordon the only member of your crew to go out onto the surface near Lowell?'

'No. Polowski and Korder went with him. But neither of them went down into the crater.'

The man gestured towards two of the men as he spoke. 'They remained in sight of the crawler on the crater rim.'

'Was it possible for you two men to see what Gordon was doing all the time he was inside the crater?'

The two men nodded and one of them — Naysmith later learned that he was Franz Korder — said: 'We could see him all the time. The crawler was positioned so that the forward searchlight was shining directly into the crater.'

'What was he doing?'

'He seemed to be examining the rock samples on the crater floor.'

'I see. Did he handle any of them? I'd like you to be absolutely certain about this.'

Polowski jerked his head in affirmation. 'He was hoping to bring back some samples and I saw him chipping away at one or two of the boulders.'

'And did he return with any samples?'

'No.'

'You're sure of that?' Naysmith persisted.

'Certain, Doctor. He had a sealable bag with him but it was empty when he came back to the crawler.'

Naysmith felt a pang of disappointment. If only some samples had been brought back they might have learned a lot from them. Still, it was no great tragedy. He had already made up his mind to visit the crater as soon as the opportunity presented itself.

'Just one more thing. Did either of you notice anything peculiar about that particular crater? Anything at all? Strange rock formations, phosphorescence? Unusual colouring?'

Korder shrugged. 'Nothing out of the ordinary as far as I could see. However, it was still dark, about an hour before dawn and in the light from the searchlight everything was black and white. You can't make out any colour in that sort of light.'

'No, of course not.' Naysmith bit his lip. He had learned very little apart from the fact that Gordon had definitely entered the crater and handled some of the rock.

'Now,' he went on, 'is there anything you want to ask me? I can understand your position and confusion at what has happened. And believe me, no one regrets having to put you men into quarantine like this more than I do. But unfortunately it's necessary until we can get to the bottom of this crisis.'

There was silence in the quarantine dome for several moments as the men looked at each other, waiting for someone to speak. Then the leader cleared his throat and said: 'I think I'm speaking for every man here, doctor, when I ask if you know just how contagious this disease is and what our chances are.'

Naysmith had guessed that was coming and had tried to prepare for it. After all, what could you say to men in a predicament such as this? That they were almost certainly dealing with a completely alien organism, one they had never encountered before, and he didn't have an answer to that question. These men wanted reassurance and it was up to him to give it as far as he was able.

'Well, doctor?'

'As far as the degree of contagion is concerned, we don't know very much at present. We've carried out tests on rats and none of them have contracted the disease. They're still healthy and running about their cage. If they had caught the disease they would all be dead by now.'

That wasn't strictly true, he thought sharply. After all, they had literally no proof that these two men would have died if they had remained inside their suits. But it was too early in their experiments to go into that.

'And if it's any further consolation to you,' he went on quickly, 'none of the other members of that first expedition have shown any ill effects.'

'Then why did Gordon and the other man die?'

'We don't know. I'll be quite honest with you. There are so many baffling characteristics about their deaths that we'll have to explore every possibility we can think of. At the moment, we're working round the clock to try to find the answer. You can rest assured we're doing everything possible to get to the bottom of this thing.'

There were no further questions and five minutes later Naysmith was on his way to the Pathology lab. It was as he was making his way along the wide outer corridor that he suddenly realised what had been nagging at his mind for the past half hour.

Two men!

Both had presumably left their vehicles to examine the crater floor of Lowell on foot. Both had, if their diagnosis was correct, been infected by some Martian organism.

Yet both had, quite obviously, been wearing protective suits all the time. Suits that were specifically designed to exclude any leakage of air, as completely impenetrable as they could possibly be.

70

Yet somehow, the organism had succeeded in penetrating them. There seemed no other alternative.

Before he could tell this to Corval, there came the sound of hurrying footsteps echoing hollowly on the floor of the corridor. A moment later, Schwartzwald came running towards him.

'Where's Major Brander?'

Naysmith pointed behind him. 'In the control room questioning those men who just arrived. Why, what's happened?'

'We've just had a report there's an interplanetary ship coming in. An unscheduled flight from Earth. A party of top-ranking politicians on a fact-finding visit.'

'Oh Christ,' Naysmith muttered as Schwartzwald ran past him without stopping. 'That really does it. We can't allow them to land here in the middle of this crisis!'

4

The dawn light of Mars filtered through the wide window of the Pathology lab, looking directly out onto the pitted surface outside. It was dull at first, little more than a faint brightening of the overall darkness, but it grew brighter. Slender pinnacles of rock that marked the rim of a small crater nearby stood out on the horizon as the last of the stars dimmed.

From where he stood, Naysmith could now pick out more details of the landscape. In some ways it resembled the Moon with which he was familiar. But there were obvious differences. On the Moon, everything was stark and angled, a monochrome of white and black with no in-between shades. Here there was plenty of colour and the various rock formations had a softer, weathered look about them.

Beyond the furthest dome, a long, shallow depression ran worm-like across

72

the desert. It looked like an ancient riverbed but whether, as some astronomers believed, it had once carried water far back in the history of Mars, was debatable.

I wonder if there'll ever come a time when we make this planet green and habitable like Earth, he thought, watching the bright disc of the sun creep into sight over the crater rim. We can't live forever under these domes, only about to walk the surface in the protection of our suits. Or maybe there'll be a process like that far back on Earth when the fishes came out of the shallow seas and walked on the land; when those born here on Mars succeed in adapting themselves to that thin atmosphere. Then they'll be Martians and no longer have any ties with Earth.

He turned away and walked back to where Corval was performing the autopsy, working with an infinite patience. Most of the vital organs had already been removed for further study. But it had been a long and tedious job, made more difficult by the fact that he had to work from behind the thick glass shield using the same kind of mechanical manipulators that were normally employed for handling radioactive materials.

By an elaborate system of reduction gearing, large-scale movements of his hands were transformed into minute movements of scalpels, retractors and other surgical instruments.

'Isn't this rather difficult?' Naysmith asked.

'It is,' Corval agreed. 'Unfortunately there's no other way of carrying out such an operation. We have to avoid the risk of any further spread of the disease by all means possible.'

'I suppose it is possible that a dead body can no longer transmit the infection. I'm thinking of it more in terms of a virus rather than a bacterium. One that can live only for a short time outside a life-host. Once that host dies, the virus dies too.'

'Is that likely?' Corval looked round.

'Normally — no. Such a virus would soon die out completely if it persisted in killing off its hosts. But don't forget we're dealing with an alien organism. We know absolutely nothing of its life-cycle at all.

We don't even know if it's made up of the same proteins and amino-acids as those we're used to dealing with on Earth.'

Corval was silent, evidently turning that over in his mind. Then he gave a grunt of satisfaction and stepped away from the controls.

'That's as much as I can do here. Now all we have to do is examine everything. Prepare frozen sections, make up slides for staining. The electron microscope will be a useful tool if we are dealing with a virus.'

'It's a lot of work,' Naysmith agreed as Corval flexed his stiff fingers. 'If I can operate the electron microscope it may help.'

The doctor nodded briefly. 'I'm intrigued by your hypothesis regarding the size of the causative agent. If we assume that the suits in use by the men on the surface are leak proof against air we must be dealing with something almost on the atomic or molecular level.'

'And you find that hard to believe?'

'Yes. I feel it must have gained entry through the suits in a perfectly logical manner. If we're forced to examine more fantastic possibilities we'll make little headway at all. We'll be sidetracked all over the place with so many red herrings thrown in that we'll never solve this problem.'

'That's true — but only up to a point. It's quite likely we may have to scrap all our preconceived notions entirely.'

Naysmith left Corval to carry on with his work and went back to the smaller laboratory that housed the electron microscope. As he pushed open the door it was thrust against him from the other side.

Carine Wilder said hurriedly: 'Sorry, John. Brander has been on the communicator for you. Wants to see both of us right away. I told him where Doctor Corval is and he's contacting him right now.'

Naysmith sighed. What the hell was it this time? There seemed to have been nothing but one crisis following close on the heels of another ever since he had arrived. How were they expected to get on with the crucial task of identifying this lethal agent with these constant interruptions?

★ ★ ★

As soon as they entered the Security office, Brander said tightly: 'This won't take long. I realise how valuable your time is. I just want to inform you that I've put Directive SB-17-5Z into operation as of five minutes ago.'

'And what exactly does that mean?' Naysmith asked.

'It means this entire base is now isolated. No one can enter or leave under any circumstances. I've informed that incoming vessel carrying those politicians. They're now in closed orbit around Mars and there they'll stay until this is cleared up, one way or another. That was also the last communication to leave this base. No incoming messages will be acknowledged.'

'You realise those politicians will have informed Earth of what has happened?'

'I'm aware of that. Theoretically we could have blanketed their entire communication system and jammed any broadcast. But that may only have made matters worse than they are at present.'

'And what about the rest of the people on the base?' Naysmith looked up as he spoke, watching the security chief's face, 'Have you told them?'

Brander hesitated. Then he shook his head. 'No. I thought that not only unnecessary at the present time but also undesirable. I don't want to spread panic throughout the colony.'

'So long as there are no deaths outside the quarantine block, you might get away with it. But if this should spread — '

Brander's features were set into grim lines. His face was white and he looked more like a corpse at that moment than a living man. Then he said, 'If it should spread and show signs of getting out of control, we have no alternative but to initiate Directive Sterilisation AB-6. Doctor Corval here knows what that means.'

Corval's face was like stone as he stared straight in front of him. Carefully, he formed the words. 'It means the total destruction of the entire base by means of nuclear devices.'

'You mean there are nuclear bombs inside the base?' Carine's tone was incredulous, her eyes wide.

Brander nodded his head wearily. The lines across his forehead seemed to have deepened over the last few seconds. 'There are five nuclear bombs buried some seven hundred metres under this site. All of them are situated at strategic points and all linked to the central computer.'

'But why?' she persisted.

Brander placed his thin-fingered hands flat on the desk. He stared intently at them for a long moment as if trying to find some reasonable explanation from his scrutiny of his fingers.

Lifting his head, he said thinly. 'For just such a contingency as this. We're on a completely unknown world, Miss Wilder. This is not Earth or even Luna. We know that it's possible for life forms to come into existence in this environment, alien life forms. These devices will contain any outbreak of an epidemic nature. They are scheduled to remain there for a period of at least ten years. By that time, it is hoped we will have been able to prove, quite conclusively, that no danger to human life exists on Mars.'

'And how are the bombs activated?' Naysmith put in. He felt suddenly cold although the room was warm.

The security man smiled frostily. 'There's no need to alarm yourself, doctor. Directive Sterilization AB-6 requires three coded instructions to be programmed simultaneously into the computer by Doctor Corval, Schwartzwald and myself. Once set in operation, however, it cannot be reversed or cancelled.'

'I see,' Naysmith pursed his lips. 'You seem to have thought of everything.'

'We hope so.'

★　★　★

Naysmith rubbed his eyes wearily and stared at the picture on the rectangular screen above the electron microscope. He was, he realised, looking at a picture of part of the dead man's lung, only a very thin sliver it was true, and magnified more than half a million diameters.

Carine Wilder, standing beside the bench, said, 'Find anything?'

He stepped back a couple of paces from the screen. 'No. Nothing there that has no right to be.'

'It just doesn't make sense.'

'That's what I keep telling myself. This entire affair has got me completely baffled. You know, I'm beginning to think we've been on the wrong track all the time. There is no bacterium, no virus.'

'Then what is it?'

'I only wish to God I knew. Mass hallucination. Some form of self-hypnosis. A new type of radiation we've never come across before. Your guess is as good as mine, Carine.'

'You're tired. I doubt if you've had a proper night's rest since you got here.'

She took his arm and made him sit down on one of the benches. 'I'll brew up some coffee. You've been staring at that screen for the best part of two hours.'

'Thanks. Maybe Corval is having better luck than we are. We have to get a break sometime,' he reflected wearily. 'We can't just go on stumbling around in the dark getting nowhere.' More strongly than ever, he had the feeling that they had somehow missed a vital piece of evidence. The answer was staring them in the face if only they could recognise it.

'Here, drink this.' Carine stood beside him, a mug of steaming coffee in her right hand. There was an expression of instant concern on her regular features. 'Then I think you should get a few hours sleep.'

'But there's still so much to do and — '

'And you'll be in no condition to do it unless you get some rest. Doctor Corval won't have any result much before morning and as you just said, we're not getting much information here. When did you last get more than an hour's rest?'

Naysmith sipped his coffee, then forced a quick grin. 'It seems so long ago I can't really remember.'

'There you are then.' Her tone brooked no argument. 'Finish your coffee and then bunk down in your room. I'll call you if anything turns up.'

'Promise?'

'I promise.' She stood with her back

against the side of the bench, resting her weight on her arms. She watched him thoughtfully while he drank the scalding coffee slowly. Then she took the mug from him.

'Off you go.' She took his arm and led him towards the door. 'You look dead beat. Once you've rested you'll be able to tackle this problem with a fresh mind. In the meantime, I'll hold the fort.'

'Thanks.' He smiled gratefully. For the first time he realised how utterly weary he was. This was not the sort of field trip he had visualised when he had embarked on the planetship at Aristarchus. Things were happening so quickly that his mind was refusing to take them all in.

A few minutes later, he opened the door of his room and went inside. He did not bother to switch on the light but took off his jacket and shoes in the warm darkness. Then he stretched himself out on the low bunk against the curved wall and stared up at the almost invisible ceiling.

In spite of the utter weariness in his limbs, his mind was still alert, throwing up questions he could not answer. For a little while he let his thoughts roam freely. He tried to recall everything he knew about viruses. Many of them were specific in that they attacked only a certain organ of the body whereas others were much more generalised in their mode of attack. Carefully, he tried to marshal all the facts he had, visualising them in his mind.

Two dead men.

Both had complained of intense headaches. Both had apparently gone insane before they had, to all intents and purposes, committed suicide.

Now why would a man deliberately go to the trouble of making his way up through the various levels of the Base until he was at ground level and then manually open one of the airlocks, knowing that once he took a single step outside without a suit he would die within seconds? Or that other man in the crawler. He had removed his suit which must have taken some little time and trouble, opened the rear exit of the vehicle and jumped out.

It didn't make sense. Two men separated by weeks and in somewhat different situations, yet they had both gone to their deaths in almost identical ways. There had to be a link somewhere between the two.

He was suddenly too tired to think further. Turning over onto his side he fell asleep almost immediately.

★ ★ ★

A pale greyish-yellow light was filtering through the small transparent port when he awoke and there was a faint sound that he couldn't quite place. He rubbed his eyes and swung his legs to the floor. For some reason he had resisted waking up but now, with the hard coldness of the floor under his feet, he was wide awake.

He realised that the sound he could hear was a dust storm hammering against the side of the dome. The sun was up but completely hidden behind the thick cloud of whirling, flying grains. Sometimes these storms could last for several days before they finally blew themselves out and he felt suddenly glad that Directive SB 17-5Z had been invoked. By now, all of the exploring teams should be in.

It had been known for a crawler and its crew to be lost when caught in such storms, the driver wandering around in circles until their air or food supplies ran out.

Pulling on his shoes he swiftly remembered the thoughts that had been in his mind just before he had fallen asleep. Glancing at his watch he saw that he had slept for almost eight hours. He experienced a sudden sense of alarm. He hadn't intended to sleep so long. With events moving as quickly as they had over the past couple of days there was no telling what had been happening while he had been asleep.

Pulling on his jacket, he walked quickly to the Pathology lab and thrust open the door. Carine glanced up from the electron microscope with a start, then relaxed. She smiled warmly.

'Feeling any better, John?'

'Why did you let me sleep so long? It's been more than eight hours.'

'You needed it. Besides, there was no need to wake you.'

He stood beside her and glanced at the screen above the instrument.

Already, his thoughts were returning to their usual channels. 'Have you found anything yet?'

Carine's face registered disappointment. 'Nothing.' She swung around on the chair. 'I've been scanning most of the sections. If I didn't know any better, I'd say that man was perfectly healthy. That he ought to be alive now.'

Naysmith wondered briefly what they could be looking for. A strange virus? If that were so, it ought to have shown up under the magnification they were using. Even something only a few molecules in diameter would be clearly visible.

'So there's nothing showing. Just where does that leave us?'

Carine shrugged. 'I only wish I knew. Right at the very beginning, I'd say.'

'And nothing from Corval?'

'He was in a couple of times during the night. I told him you were resting. I gather he can find nothing either.'

Lowering himself into the other seat, Naysmith ran his fingers over the smooth metal of the electron microscope. He found himself staring at the image on the screen. His thoughts were chaotic but with an effort he forced himself to think logically and clearly.

Those two dead men. Either they had been running from something, or towards something they believed they had seen. That suggested some form of hallucinatory symptom that had —

He halted his thoughts at that particular moment and slammed his clenched fist hard on top of the bench, rattling the assembled glassware.

'My God,' he said harshly. 'What a bloody fool I've been.' Carine looked at him in sudden surprise. 'Are you all right, John?'

'I think I've got the answer. Well, a part of it at least. I'll have to talk with Corval right away. If I'm right, then it explains why we've failed to find the organism so far.'

Carine puckered her brows. Then she swung herself out of the chair. 'I'll get him up here right away.'

As soon as he arrived, Corval said,

'You've found something, John?'

'Not exactly. I've just realised something; something that we've completely overlooked. Yet it's been under our noses all the time.'

'What is it?'

'That first man who died. Don't you remember his eyes? How all of the colour had been bleached from the pupils.'

'Why, of course! Then it is a virus and it's highly specific. Probably only attacks the humours of the eye, or perhaps even the optic nerve.'

'Looks like that to me. We've been examining all the vital organs except those that carry the disease.'

'Then that's easily remedied.' Corval seemed suddenly excited, almost elated. 'I'll culture one of the optic nerves right away. Better retain the other in case we want an electron micrograph.'

'Can you arrange that as quickly as possible. I want to put some questions to the computer.'

Corval eyed him quizzically. 'You working on a theory or just a hunch?'

'Call it a hunch for the moment. I'll

probably know a little more once I get the answers to these questions that have been bugging me.'

'Let me know right away if you find anything that could give us a lead,' Corval said, turning towards the door. 'We'll have Brander breathing down our necks again very soon. Those politicians in orbit out there won't be liking this situation one little bit. And once they discover that none of their transmissions to the Base are being answered, they'll automatically think the worst. Besides, even if the cultures or the electron micrographs show us something to enable us to identify this organism, we still have to set about trying to find an antidote for it.'

'Would you like me to come with you and help with the computer programme, John?' Carine asked. 'I've operated the one we have on the base for nearly a year. I can set in the necessary programme for you.'

'That would help tremendously. I'm a little rusty myself where these things are concerned.'

The central computer was situated some

way off the main system of corridors in a large, air-conditioned room. Two technicians were already working it when Naysmith and the girl entered. They glanced up briefly, then went back to their duties. For a moment, Naysmith wondered whether either of them realised the enormity of the disaster that might face them if the small team, of which he was one, failed in their task.

Then the thought faded out as he walked across to the large console, he felt the pressure of time on his shoulders like an invisible hand, clamping more tightly with every hour that passed.

That planetship out there in orbit around Mars unable to land while this biological crisis remained was one big problem they still had to face. Certainly those on board could survive for a long time but there would soon be pressures coming to bear from the Government on Earth.

By now they would have received that message sent out from the ship warning them of trouble on Mars. What they would eventually decide to do was anyone's guess at the moment but it was doubtful if they would remain idle for long.

He settled himself in one of the chairs in front of the console, staring at the immense machine for a long moment, taking it all in.

Then Carine said, 'Perhaps if you tell me what you have in mind, John.'

He nodded briefly. 'At the moment I can only go on past experience and that may not be enough. But first of all I'd like to know every kind of symptom that may be produced by some bacterium or virus that attacks the optic nerve of a human being.'

'Just a human being?' She raised her brows a little. 'Why not generalise for any form of life?'

'Because as far as we know, those two rats were not affected. That may be because they're somehow immune to this disease. Or it may be that the symptoms produced are different in their case.'

'I understand.' She did not question him further but began punching information into the computer.

At last the programme was set.

'This should take only a few seconds.'

The instrument hummed quietly to itself. The computer could work out problems in seconds that would take a team of mathematicians several hours or days. It was just the feeding in of the relevant data that took up most of the time. Because of this, several operators were able to use it at the same time and it was rarely out of operation.

Letters and words formed on the display screen, and Carine snatched at the automatic print-out and handed it to him, glancing over his shoulder as he scanned it rapidly, a growing sense of excitement in him.

The answer was quite clear.

There were two main kinds of symptoms that would be introduced under the conditions he had specified. The first was varying degrees of blindness depending upon the severity of the damage done. The second — and it was this he had been hoping for — was the production of intense hallucinations that might take a number of forms.

'That's it,' he said tautly.

'So you think those two men suffered hallucinations which made them commit suicide?'

'In a way — yes. But they didn't commit suicide. And what else but an hallucination would make a man run away from the safety of the dome or the crawler and run out into the atmosphere of Mars?'

'But is it possible for an hallucination to be as intense, as compelling, as that?'

'I think so. I'm no authority on the subject. Corval can answer that better than I can.'

Naysmith found himself recalling a paper he had read in his college days — a very old paper if he remembered correctly by a member of the London Society for Psychical Research dealing with the subject of ghosts. Funny he should recall it at this particular moment but there had been something in it that now seemed very relevant to the problem they were facing here.

In it, the author had put forward the suggestion that ghosts and similar apparitions existed only in the minds of those who claimed to have seen them. Everyone who visited a place reputed to be haunted knew something of the background of such hauntings and under the extremely emotional conditions that prevailed at the time, it was highly probable the person concerned formed an image of the so-called ghost in his brain.

Somehow, though by what means it was impossible to tell, the brain reversed the normal sequence of seeing. The usual process was for the eye to form an image, which was then transmitted along the bundle of optic nerves to the brain where it was reformed. Under these very special circumstances, however, the brain formed the picture first and then sent the electrical impulses back along the optic nerve to the eye.

Perhaps this was something similar, only it was the action of this alien organism that provided the necessary stimulus.

He felt suddenly very excited. If he was right, then such an organism should show up quite clearly on the electron micro-scope. There might also be evidence of the kind of damage done to the optic nerve.

It wouldn't be all of the answer, of course. Only the beginning. But any clue at all would be more than welcome now — anything to give them a lead.

There were still a lot of oddities about this disease they did not yet understand. On the surface, from what little evidence they had, it did not seem to be contagious. Only one member of each of the crews had been affected although it was true that in each case it had been the man who had actually got out of the crawler to investigate that particular crater region.

In addition, even if they did succeed in finding it they still had to identify it, if possible, and then find some suitable, and rapid-acting, antidote.

An hour later, Corval had prepared a dozen culture plates.

These had been incubated under a variety of atmospheres, pressures and temperatures to simulate Earthlike and Martian conditions.

Carine brought them out of the

thermostatted ovens and placed them on the bench under one of the lights.

Corval ran a practised eye over them. Then: 'Nothing there at all as far as I can see,' he said tonelessly. He glanced in Naysmith's direction. 'Is this what you expected?'

'Far from it.' Naysmith shook his head emphatically. He tried to keep the disappointment out of his voice. 'I'd hoped that at least one would have shown something.'

'We can scan them under the light microscope if you like, just in case there is something.'

'All right.'

Twenty minutes later they knew for certain that there was nothing growing on the nutrient media.

'The only explanation I can think of is that this organism just won't multiply on any of the media we're using.'

'That's possible I suppose.' Corval scratched his chin. 'It fits in with one of the facts we know.'

'What's that?'

'Since this base has been in existence,'

Corval said slowly, 'we've had more than fifty expeditions out to various areas of the planet, some of them ranging as far afield as five hundred kilometres from here. So far, only those two that have gone to Lowell have brought back the disease. If that means — and I think it does — that it's somehow specific for that particular region, then we'll have to do a lot of rethinking.'

'About the sort of medium on which it can exist?'

'That — and also if there are any peculiar, possibly unique, conditions around that crater. That will be something for the astronomy and geology boys to chew over. They might be able to come up with something.'

'I think I'll get on to them right away. How long will it take to prepare a section of optic nerve for the electron microscope?'

Corval glanced at his watch. 'About half an hour, possibly a little longer.'

'Okay. Then give me an hour and I'll join you there. In the meantime I want to go over to the observatory.'

5

Perhaps the most significant thing about Martin Freeman was that he knew more about Mars than he did about Earth, which was his home planet. Indeed, he often said that all he knew of Earth was that it was the larger and brighter of the magnificent double system that shone so brightly in the Martian sky.

Physically, he was a tall, slight man, with a pronounced stoop that added to, rather than detracted from, his height.

The Syrtis observatory was situated apart from the complex of dome-like structures of the Base on an elevated region of the surface away from the craters that dotted this region. Like all of the outlying buildings, the Astronomy Department was reached by a long tunnel shielded by a curved laminated plastic that gave a strangely distorted view of the surrounding terrain.

It was here, in the observatory, that

Naysmith found the astronomer. He was not at all surprised by the other's appearance. Freeman was dressed in a loose-fitting red shirt, open at the neck, and a pair of rumpled, stained trousers. On his feet was a pair of open-toed plastic sandals.

The telescope, which took up most of the circular observatory, was an exceptionally well-designed piece of instrumentation. With the setting up of astronomical observatories on Luna and Mars, the engineers had been faced with a fresh set of problems unlike any they had encountered before.

The forty-inch refractor was hermetically sealed into the spherical dome in such a manner that the entire framework of the dome moved in any direction with the telescope. In a like manner, the objective glass was directly sealed into the tube so that it was possible for the operator to use the instrument without the need of protective clothing. The atmosphere inside the room remained sealed in and the unbreathable Martian atmosphere could not enter.

Some of the associated problems had

taxed the ingenuity of the engineers to the limit. In particular, since the dome was a perfect sphere, with one half moving beneath the floor, it had been necessary to design its motion so that it rotated with the minimum of friction and, in spite of the lower Martian gravity, the entire dome and telescope weighed close on twenty tons, all of which moved smoothly at the touch of a button.

Freeman listened attentively as Naysmith outlined the position to him. The rather mournful expression on his long, lined face did not change.

'Two men dead already,' he said finally, running a finger along the bridge of his nose. 'This is the first I've heard of it although I know Brander has put Directive SB 17-5Z into operation. I didn't know his reasons for it. But then, we're rarely brought into any of these decisions. People tend to forget we're here.' He smiled faintly but there was no mirth in the twitch of his lips.

'In the circumstances I gather there was little else he could do.'

'Of course. I understand that now. But

how do you think I can be of any help? Surely this is a purely biological affair.'

'Not entirely. We thought so too at first. Now we think there may be more to it than that. It seems the only source of these organisms that we know of is the region around one particular crater.'

Freeman raised thick, bushy brows. 'Oh. Which one is that?'

'Lowell. Not far from here.'

'I see.' A frown crossed the other's features. 'Somehow, I'm not too surprised.'

'Then there is something different about that particular crater?'

Without replying, the astronomer got up and went over to a map on the wall. He jabbed at it with a long forefinger. 'There's the base — and here's Lowell. Not a very conspicuous formation even as Martian craters go, is it?'

The map was extraordinarily well detailed, unlike any other of the Martian surface Naysmith had seen. There were hundreds of horizontal, vertical, diagonal and curving lines on it, cross-hatching to produce what was almost a three-dimensional effect. He looked closely at

Lowell but as Freeman had said, there seemed little to differentiate it from the hundreds of other craters dotted around the base.

'Then what's so strange about it?'

The other forced a quick smile. 'Do you know anything about the current theories concerning the origin of the Martian craters?'

'Very little, I'm afraid.'

Freeman motioned him to a chair. 'Sit down. I'll try to explain the ideas as briefly as I can. As in the case of the Moon, there are two rival theories, namely meteoric bombardment and some form of vulcanisn. There is a third idea which combines the two. This is that a meteor, striking the surface with a high velocity, penetrates quite deeply before all of its momentum is spent. In so doing, it gassifies some of the surrounding rock, at the same time raising the temperature by several thousand degrees. We then have the formation of a bubble of gas trapped beneath the detritus formed by the initial impact.'

'And this, in turn, can force its way to

the surface and produce a crater?'

'Exactly. There was a feeling a long time ago that the presence of an atmosphere on Mars might produce marked frictional burning of any incoming meteorites. We now know that the atmosphere is sufficiently tenuous for such an effect to be only marginal.'

'Go on.'

'One strange feature we find about the Martian craters which is not prevalent on the lunar surface is that many of them are present in the form of chains of craters, lying in almost perfectly straight lines across the surface. It seems highly improbable that these could be caused by meteoric bombardment since it would imply that a flight of meteors came in, one after the other, at regular intervals, spaced out by minutes only, perhaps even seconds.'

'So these would have been formed by some kind of volcanic action?'

'That's what we believe. In addition, these craters appear to be of approximately the same age. Lowell, on the other hand, is undoubtedly of meteoric origin.

So far as I'm aware, this has been agreed by everyone concerned. It's also one of the youngest craters we know of, certainly not more than a few hundred years old at the outside. Indeed, there's fairly strong evidence that it did not exist at the time of the first Mariner flypasts of the planet.'

'The presumption being that Lowell is not only the youngest of all Martian craters but it was also caused by a meteor hitting the surface.'

'That would appear to be the logical conclusion.'

'So if there's a pocket of organic life out there, it may conceivably have come from within this meteorite and not be an indigenous Martian life form?'

'Don't you consider that possible?'

Naysmith shrugged. 'Certainly there have been several claims in the past to have discovered bacteria in meteorites which landed on Earth. Most of the early ones didn't stand up to scientific investigation and examination showed these organisms to be Earth contaminants. But a few of the later investigations of carbonaceous meteorites were carried out under very stringent conditions to eliminate every possibility of contamination by normal terrestrial organisms. The results I've seen published show very peculiar organisms unlike any known on Earth.'

'There is another alternative, of course.'

'What's that?'

'Well, it's more in your province than mine. But from what we know of Mars, this is a world in which life may be just about to come into being. The atmosphere is somewhat like that of ancient Earth in its composition. What exists around Lowell may be the first attempt at life on this planet.'

'That doesn't fit in with any of our present theories on the origin of life.' Naysmith said pointedly after digesting the other's remark. 'If life came into existence on Mars, or will come into existence at some time, in a way similar to that which we believe happened on Earth, it would require some very special conditions. For example, is there any evidence for the presence of water around Lowell?'

Freeman pursed his lips in concentration. 'None that I know of. But you must remember we're still on the verge of exploring that region. That's why there have been only a few expeditions to Lowell so far.'

'Were any of those men carrying out specific investigations for your department?'

'I'd hoped to get some information back from them, it's true. I certainly never expected this to happen. How serious is it?'

'I don't want to cause any alarm, but it could prove to be extremely serious. We have a number of men confined in quarantine and we can't keep them there forever. The members of that first team are loose inside the base and for all we know there may be carriers of the disease among them. If there are, we could soon have a full-scale epidemic on our hands. And to cap it all, there's a planetship full of important politicians in orbit around Mars unable to land while this crisis is with us.'

Freeman whistled through his teeth. 'I'd no idea it was as bad as that. And you haven't isolated this organism yet, I presume?'

'No. Everything we've tried so far has been a complete failure with negative results all along the line.'

'Well, if there's any further help I can give you, don't hesitate to come along and ask. I'm always glad of company and you'll find me here most of the time.'

'Thanks. I've a feeling I'll take you up on that.'

★ ★ ★

By the time Naysmith arrived back in the Pathology lab Corval had prepared sections using a microtome which shaved off thin slices of the optic nerve only a score or so molecules in thickness. The area around the electron microscope was cramped due to the bulk of the instrument.

'We're almost ready,' Corval said, without turning his head. 'As you've seen this particular instrument has an image-resolution attachment which will enable us to view the specimen directly. Rather like a television screen in many ways. We can also scan the section, which may be a big help.'

As he spoke he lifted the thin wafer on its mounting with a pair of delicate forceps and placed it in the small metal cap which then went inside the instrument.

'Did you get anything useful from old Freeman, by the way?'

'Yes, although I'm not sure yet how it fits in with what we've found. Apparently Lowell is only around a hundred years old if we can believe the evidence from the first Mariner probes. That, in itself, indicates it's one of the most likely sites on the planet where something odd might occur.'

'Then you're thinking of the meteoric hypothesis,' said Carine, glancing in his direction.

Naysmith permitted himself a brief nod. 'It might provide the answers to a lot of the puzzles associated with this disease.'

'But wouldn't the heat generated by the friction as it came down through the atmosphere burn up anything organic?'

'It would near the surface of a meteorite. But if these organisms were in the centre, then things might be different. A stony meteorite would be an excellent insulator.'

'He's right, Carine,' put in Corval. 'In a way, I'm surprised they never found organic life on the Moon below the surface. The dust layer there would insulate them from the extreme range of temperature.'

Carine checked the controls, then said: 'Didn't someone suggest that life on Earth originated in cometary debris which intersected the Earth's orbit millions of years ago?'

'That's right. Hoyle and his colleagues put forward the idea way back in the twentieth century.'

'Do you think it's possible?'

'Perhaps. If we find anything out near Lowell we may even furnish the first actual proof of this hypothesis.'

There was a faint throb as Corval started the vacuum pump, to evacuate the electron microscope. Unlike the ordinary optical microscope, this instrument used a beam of electrons to delineate the outlines of the object being examined and for this reason, it was necessary to have as near perfect a vacuum inside the instrument as possible.

The major advantage of the electron microscope was that the wavelength of an electron is much shorter than that of visible light enabling it to outline smaller regions with a high degree of resolution. Magnifications of up to a million diameters were now readily attainable.

Once the instrument had been pumped down, Corval manipulated the controls, focussing the beam.

'All right, Carine. Douse the lights,' he said quietly. 'Then we'll take a look at what we have here.'

'If anything,' Naysmith added softly.

The room was plunged into darkness as Carine switched off the overhead lights. Then, on the rectangular screen, the image came swiftly into focus.

Naysmith leaned forward and peered intently at the picture outlined there. He felt suddenly warm inside and tremendously excited.

It was all there.

Indeed, it was far clearer than he had

imagined it would be.

There was the thick branch of the optic nerve running diagonally across the screen and, wound around it like a string of incredibly thin wire, was something that glowed with an eerie green.

'Well, there it is,' Corval said in a hushed tone. 'I don't think there can be much doubt about that. But I've certainly never seen anything like it before.'

'It can't be more than two or three molecules in diameter,' Naysmith said. He traced the outline with his finger. 'But it must be several hundred, possibly a thousand or so in length.'

Carine looked over his shoulder, her face a pale blue in the faint illumination. 'Notice too those irregularities on the optic nerve structure just around it. They must be due to some kind of systematic damage to the nerve.'

'See if you can scan along it,' Naysmith suggested.

Deftly, Corval brushed his fingertips along one of the dials.

The picture shifted as he followed the contours of the optic nerve.

There were other, similar, wire-like lengths of the virus wrapped around it at intervals.

Straightening a little, Naysmith let his breath go in little pinches through his mouth. 'It doesn't seem to have any crystalline structure like most of the terrestrial viruses. That could explain how it was able to penetrate a spacesuit. An object only a molecule or so in diameter could conceivably enter through a defect in the suit far too small to be noticeable.'

'Certainly a defect that would cause no noticeable change in air pressure,' Corval agreed.

'So now we finally know what it looks like,' said Carine. 'And we have an idea how it can penetrate a protective suit. But how far does that get us?'

'Not very far at the moment. I doubt if it can exist symbiotically with humans. We're probably too alien for such an existence as far as the organism is concerned.'

'Meaning?'

'Meaning that it's possibly no longer alive in the sense that we can apply such a term to things like viruses.'

'I think we can also go on the assumption that the human body can't produce antibodies against such a virus,' Corval commented.

'Perhaps a broad-spectrum antibiotic,' suggested Naysmith.

'That's the only thing we have which may give us a chance of controlling it.'

Corval continued the scan for several minutes, then straightened up. 'We may be lucky. If this organism exists only in that one specific region around Lowell and if, as we think, it isn't highly contagious, then we may be able to prevent any recurrence of this disease. At least we may be able to buy ourselves a little time for further study.'

'That,' said Naysmith grimly, 'seems to depend upon an awful lot of 'ifs'.'

It was not going to be long before he realised just how right he was.

*   *   *

They worked throughout the afternoon, pausing only for something to eat in the

114

canteen, before resuming their research. By the time they had taken several photographs of the organism it was almost eight o' clock local time. The enlargements that magnified the virus a little over a million times, still showed no indication of any crystalline structure. As far as they were able to ascertain, it consisted simply of a chain of molecules, which, in many respects, were even more complex than the tobacco mosaic virus and similar organisms that had been known for more than a century.

'Do you see those odd indentations along it?' Naysmith said.

He rubbed his eyes tiredly. The lids were beginning to sting from looking too long, and too closely, at the screen. 'What do you think they could be?'

'Some form of segmentation, perhaps,' Carine suggested. She stood beside the bench with three cups of coffee balanced on a tray.

'Possibly. But to me they suggest some kind of function.'

Corval put the photograph they had been studying beside the tray. 'They may even be associated with reproduction.'

'Or growth.'

'Yes.' Corval frowned. 'I'd give anything to know if our friends here are still capable of transmitting this disease.'

'The rats indicated they're not,' said Carine. She handed a cup to Naysmith.

As he sipped the coffee, Naysmith scanned the pile of photographs. He said slowly, 'That's what worries me. From what we know of viruses, they're usually extremely contagious. So far, we've no absolute proof those rats aren't immune to the disease. Then there's a fact that we've tended to overlook, namely that there were other men in contact with those two who died after they'd returned from Lowell. None of these men appear to have contracted the disease. Why? We can't say that they're all immune. Yet theoretically, they should have caught it by now.'

Corval finished his coffee. 'I've got the feeling that we're overlooking a great many things, you know. Are we to assume that once the host is dead, the organism is harmless?'

'That could explain most of our observations.' Naysmith frowned.

'Something the matter?' asked Carine.

Naysmith was thinking, trying to remember something he had all but forgotten. Something about the human eye. For a moment he thought he had it but then the thought slipped away and he could no longer grasp the fleeting little idea.

He pinched the bridge of his nose between his fingers. His eyes ached and there was a tense tiredness across his temples. Undoubtedly, he had been staring at the screen and the photographs too long and the strain was beginning to tell on him.

'I think it's time for us to take a break,' he said finally. 'None of us is thinking straight just now. We'll simply start to go around in circles if we try to force ourselves to concentrate on the problem much longer.'

He got to his feet and made for the door, halted sharply in his tracks as the intercom on the desk buzzed peremptorily.

Carine answered it, listened for several seconds, then said tightly; 'We'll be there right away. Yes; they're both with me in the lab.'

Her face was etched into grim lines as she replaced the receiver.

'Don't tell me,' Naysmith said, wearily. 'More trouble.'

'The worst. That was Brander as you probably guessed. There have been three more cases of the Lowell Syndrome in the last twenty minutes. He wants to see us right away.'

'Damn!' Naysmith muttered the oath viciously. 'Just when we figured we might be getting somewhere — '

'At least we have one thing in our favour this time,' Corval said as they stepped out into the corridor. 'The victims can't get out of the base now that Brander has put the directive into operation.'

'That's about the only thing we've got going for us,' Naysmith grunted. He felt a surge of frustrated anger ride him as he lengthened his stride until he was almost running.

Brander was pacing the office like a caged animal when they entered, his hands clasped tightly behind his back. He looked like a man on the verge of exploding.

'All right,' he snarled hoarsely, 'I guess you know the problem so I won't waste time explaining it to you. Three more victims of this bloody disease. Where in God's name is it going to end?'

He threw himself down into his chair as he spoke, staring up at the ceiling.

Naysmith knew that the security chief had been turning over in his mind the fact that he might soon have to put Directive Sterilisation AB-6 into operation, thereby wiping out the entire base and its occupants. The thought must have been preying on his mind for several hours and this new event had brought the possibility very close.

'Any of these victims been in contact with either of the others?' Corval asked.

Brander shook his head. 'Goddamnit, I can't say for certain. But we can establish

119

no direct connection. Certainly not with the last one. All of those men from the last expedition are still in quarantine.'

'So we must now accept the fact that the virus is running wild within the base,' said Naysmith. His numbed senses told him that this was what he had always feared, that when he looked at the position objectively, it had always been on the cards. Nevertheless, the news had a shattering effect on him.

Brander lowered his gaze and stared directly at him. For a moment, there was a faint gleam of hope at the back of his eyes.

'Have you discovered the cause of the disease?'

Naysmith nodded. 'We think so. No, we're fairly certain of it. It's some form of virus that shows a remarkable predilection for the optic nerve. Such specificity isn't unknown. There are several organisms that behave in the same way.'

'And you've actually isolated this one?' Brander pulled himself upright in his chair.

'Yes.' It was Corval who answered. 'But

that doesn't solve the problem. We still have to find a cure.'

Brander's shoulders drooped visibly. 'Then we're right back where we started.'

'Not quite.' Naysmith put in. 'Because now, at least, we know that we're dealing with a definite organism. We also know certain facts about this disease which might help us.'

'Such as?'

'That some people seem to be immune to it. If the course of the Lowell Syndrome is as rapid as it would seem to be, then those men now in quarantine, and particularly those with the first expedition, should have contracted it before now. But they've not done so. This virus didn't invade their optic nerves. In fact it seems to have left them completely untouched.'

'Is that possible?'

Naysmith's eyes narrowed. 'Try to remember we're dealing with an alien organism, one which has had no previous contact with Man. Over the centuries, we've adapted to terrestrial organisms of all kinds. We can, indeed, live quite happily with more than ninety per cent of bacteria. Some of them are essential for our existence.'

'Meaning that this one is pathogenic because we haven't met with it before?'

'That's a simplified way of looking at it. Diphtheria and syphilis carried off countless victims three and four hundred years ago. Now they've adapted to us and these diseases are no longer fatal. Try to bear in mind that it's a very poor parasite that destroys its host.'

'Maybe a couple of centuries from now,' said Corval, 'this particular virus will no longer have such fatal effects. We'll simply treat it like influenza or the common cold.'

'But that's a long-term solution. It doesn't help us at the moment.'

'Is there anything at all you can do?' Brander was a man clutching at straws.

'I suppose we can try to make a serum,' Naysmith answered finally. 'And we'd better check on these latest victims. Where are they now?'

'Brander pushed back his chair. I'll take you along.'

The door said EXPERIMENTAL LABORA-TORY Q-7. Inside, the room was long and partitioned by a thick section that was set at intervals with small windows.

'This is where we carry out the preliminary experiments on any rock or soil samples brought in by the various surface expeditions,' Brander explained. 'In a way it's fortunate the three recent cases occurred close by and we were able to bring them into this laboratory. As you can see there is some form of isolation although the security isn't as stringent as in the outer quarantine sections.'

'Was any attempt made to isolate the other personnel in this area?' Corval asked, peering through one of the square windows.

Brander looked distinctly unhappy. 'I'm afraid not. Everything apparently happened so quickly there was no time for anything like that. I gave orders that everyone who came in contact with these three were to be brought here for further observation. I'm afraid that was the best I could do.'

Naysmith did not argue. He could recognise the difficulties under which Brander laboured. Most people considered that, in an isolated and strictly contained unit such as Syrtis Base, it would be a relatively simple matter to quarantine all suspects. In actual fact, one could only contain them within the perimeter of the base itself.

Little subdivision was possible. There was too much intercourse between the various factions and by the time the presence of a disease such as this was recognised and confirmed within the community, it was usually much too late to do any more than Brander had done already.

Bending, he glanced through one of the windows into the other half of the laboratory. At first he could make out nothing beyond an assortment of benches and glove boxes used for the aseptic handling of materials. Then something moved near the far wall and he realized there were three figures lying on the floor.

'It was necessary for us to strap them down,' Brander said as Naysmith turned and glanced questioningly in his direction. 'The symptoms are exactly the same as in both previous cases. They became hysterical, tried to reach one of the airlocks. Then they found the airlocks were all secured and hammered on to them until their hands were bleeding. We had to restrain them otherwise they would have done themselves serious injury. That's a measure of this insanity that seems to have taken a hold on them.'

'How long since these attacks began?'

Brander glanced at his watch. 'About thirty-five minutes, I'd say.'

Naysmith was suddenly aware of the fact that at least one of the men in the other section was mouthing words but he could hear nothing.

'Is that place soundproofed?'

Brander turned to one of the white-coated technicians beside him. The man shook his head. 'Not exactly. But the walls are pretty thick.'

'Is there any way of getting a microphone in there and hooking it up to a receiver?'

'I suppose so.' The technician looked

momentarily surprised at the request. He was undeniably frightened and kept running his tongue over lips that seemed suddenly dry.

'Then do it.'

'What do you hope to gain by that?' Brander asked as the man hurried away.

'I'm not sure. Possibly nothing. But there's one point we haven't established so far and I feel it's important.'

'What's that?' inquired Corval.

'I'd like to know whether this virus infection is lethal in itself or whether those other two men would have survived if they hadn't run out onto the surface.'

The technician came back five minutes later with a microphone hooked into a small receiver.

'If you can't get the microphone into that room tape it to one of the windows,' Corval said tautly. 'It should be sufficiently sensitive to pick up what's going on in there.'

Naysmith gave a quick nod of assent. 'Better do that, we don't want to break the seal on that place if we can help it.'

The man thrust the microphone hard

against the glass and then taped it securely in place.

'Right. Now let's see what we've got.' Naysmith switched on the receiver. Instantly, a thin, high-pitched voice spoke to them. For several seconds the words were so slurred together that it was impossible to make any sense out of them.

Then there came an audible grunt as if the speaker were struggling to break free of the restraining straitjacket that held him virtually immobile on the floor.

Then —

' . . . got to get back inside. Can't breathe . . . how in hell did I get out here in the first place . . . ?'

'He's crazy,' muttered Brander. 'Stark, raving mad.'

'Oh my God, how did this happen? Must be dreaming . . . air too thin and full of methane and . . . '

'You're right,' Corval agreed. 'He's insane.'

'Is he?' murmured Naysmith. 'I wonder.'

Corval stared at him. 'You think he's imagining that?'

'Not exactly imagining it. I think he really believes that he's out on the surface

127

and if he can get through the airlock out of the base, he'll be perfectly safe.'

'An illusion induced by the damage done to the optic nerve,' Carine said.

She had caught on quick, Naysmith thought. Inwardly, he wondered if it were a simple optical illusion that was affecting these men, or something more subtle and complex. They still weren't sure how the virus affected its host.

It could be that it rarely reversed the flow of impulses along the optic nerve, rather like that theory of ghosts in the paper he had read. No, that didn't explain it. He rejected the idea. There were too many facts against it.

Everyone attacked by this disease must have had exactly the same hallucination. So how did the virus bring about the same image in the brain of its victim, making them see the same thing. And there was no doubt this vision, illusion, call it what you like, was so intense that it subordinated all of the other senses to it.

An intelligent virus? That was utterly out of the question. Alien certainly, but intelligent — no, he refused to believe that. He tried to think straight. More and more, he had the growing impression that there were so many aspects associated with this disease that he could not begin to understand, that it was almost frightening.

Carine was speaking again and he forced himself to concentrate on what she was saying.

'I wonder if this hallucination — or whatever it is — could be powerful enough to kill them.'

'If a man believes that something can kill him strongly enough, it will. I don't think there's any doubt about that. It's the way the witchdoctors in the primitive tribes worked their so-called magic.'

'So what do we do with them?' Brander wanted to know. 'Keep them restrained so they can't cause any injury to themselves?'

'There's little else we can do at the moment. Perhaps the best thing to do is flood the place with narcothane gas. That will put them under for a few hours.'

'All right.' Corval flexed the muscles of his shoulders where a deep-seated ache had set in.

Brander cleared his throat. 'In the meantime, is there anything we can do to prevent the spread of this disease?'

Naysmith shook his head. 'Nothing, I'm afraid.' He saw the look of alarm on the security chief's face but he knew he had to be brutally frank, that the man must recognise the truth and seriousness of the situation. Because there were important decisions that would have to be made and it would be Brander, in the last analysis, who would be the man to make them.

'But we've isolated — '

'You've isolated nothing but four, no five, victims plus the men from the last expedition. What has now happened is that this organism is present in the air supply of the base. A supply that is constantly being recycled and pumped into virtually every room and laboratory.'

'I suppose you realise what you're saying, the position you're putting me in.'

'About Sterilisation AB-6?'

'Exactly. There's that ship in orbit out there with all those government politicians on board. By now, Earth will know of what has happened and they'll start to apply their own pressures. I can't afford to delay this decision much longer.'

'Corval.' Naysmith turned to the doctor. 'You're in on this decision too. What's your point of view?'

Corval looked momentarily indecisive. 'I'm forced to agree with Brander about the pressures that will soon come to bear on us. But there is one thing we mustn't lose sight of. If there is ever to be a permanent base on Mars, whether it happens to be this one or not, someone has to find the answer to this disease. At the moment, we're in the best position to find that answer. All we need is a little time.'

'How much time?' Brander snapped.

There was a pause, then Naysmith said solemnly, 'Will you give us another seventy-two hours?'

'Can you guarantee to have the solution in that time?'

'You know damned well we can't.' With an effort, Naysmith controlled his surge of anger. 'But you have to balance the possible deaths of a few more people against the death of everyone in the base once you issue that directive to the computer.'

Brander seemed on the point of arguing, then thought better of it. 'Very well,' he agreed reluctantly, 'seventy-two hours. No longer. That's all the time I can give you.'

He turned abruptly on his heel and walked away. At the door he paused as Corval said quietly:

'There's one other thing.'

'Yes?'

'I think it would be wise if you were to drop a limited thermonuclear device on Lowell.'

The security chief looked amazed. 'What?'

'You heard me. If, as we believe, that crater is the only source of this organism on the planet, the sooner it's utterly wiped out, the better.'

'I see. All right. I'll try to arrange it.' He went out, closing the door behind him.

'You think he understands the urgency of the situation where Lowell is concerned?' Carine asked.

'He'd better.' Naysmith shrugged. 'He's a very worried man. But who wouldn't be, if you had the means of total destruction in your hand and knew you had to use it very soon. I think that's why he agreed to give us more time. He's just as keen to go on living as the rest of us.'

6

For John Naysmith, there had been a certain kind of horror in listening to that quavering, frightened, high-pitched voice that had emanated from the small receiver in the experimental Laboratory. It continued to haunt and colour his thoughts during the hours that followed, hours in which he went over all of the notes and observations they had made since the crisis had broken over them.

It was there, he thought. It had to be. Somewhere here in these papers was the answer. He sat back in his chair feeling tired in spite of the amphetamines he had taken to keep himself awake. Knowing there was little time left, he had taken three of the yellow tablets — and to hell with the side effects.

Inwardly, in spite of the drug, he felt himself slowing down, his mental processes growing sluggish. A drowsiness came over him and the writing on the paper danced and blurred in front of his eyes. He reached out and shifted the lamp beside him so that more light fell upon the closely printed sheets.

Earlier, he had insisted that Carine should get some sleep. There was little to do until they had worked out some method of preparing a serum that might combat the disease. Even that was only a vague possibility, he reflected tiredly. With an organism as alien as this, there was no guarantee that the methods they normally used would work.

Riffling through the papers he came across a report from Jordan, which he recalled having previously skimmed through and then pushing on one side as having little bearing upon the immediate problem. He read through it again, more carefully this time, and as he did so, he realised they had probably made a very serious mistake.

There was an oval red stamp in the top right-hand corner that read:

THIS REPORT IS CLASSIFIED SECRET
Examination by screened personnel only.

Naysmith sat forward, resting his weight on his elbows, and began to read. Lowell had been discovered some three years earlier by one of the dozen or so mapping satellites put into orbit around Mars. Little real attention had been paid to it, however, until it had been realised that the crater had not shown up on any of the very early Mariner flypasts. After eliminating various possibilities, it had finally been concluded that the crater was, indeed, a very recent formation. As far as the astronomers were aware, it was certainly one of the youngest features on the entire planet apart from Syrtis Base itself.

There were, it appeared, two possibilities. Either Lowell was the result of a recent meteor fall just prior to the building of the base, or a bubble of gas that existed beneath the surface, which, thrusting its way up, had formed an unstable dome that had then collapsed inward. As yet, there was no definite evidence in favour of either hypothesis.

Careful thermal investigations indicated that the average ground temperature in the region of the crater was two point six degrees higher than the surrounding region. There was no measurable radioactivity and rock samples showed no marked chemical or physical abnormalities compared with others in that area.

The crater was roughly oval in shape and approximately a kilometre in diameter. The ring wall was almost complete and the rocky peaks were sharper, showing far less weathering, than the other Martian formations that had been examined in detail.

Again, thought Naysmith, that pointed to a recent origin. So apart from its obvious youth, there was very little to differentiate it from all the others.

Yet two men who had entered that crater on foot had died and the disease they had brought with them was now running wild inside the Base!

The paper included several photographs of Lowell taken from one or more of the orbiting satellites. There were also three that must have been taken by the men on that earlier expedition.

Naysmith examined them closely. On

the pictures taken by the satellites, the crater appeared as a small oval depression with the fairly well-formed ringwall showing clearly and with little sign of any erosion. The floor was reasonably smooth but strewn with large boulders, particularly around the interiors of the ringwall.

With a sigh, he turned his attention to the other photographs taken from the surface. Two had obviously been obtained from somewhere on the crater rim, looking down onto the floor. The sun had been just above the horizon at the time throwing long, irregular black shadows across the crater floor. One outstanding feature, he noticed at once. was the jagged crack that extended from one side of the crater to the other. It was far from easy to judge the true scale of the picture but he estimated the crack to be several metres across at its widest point. As for its depth, that was problematical and something at which he could only guess.

It was the third picture, however, that intrigued him most. It had clearly been taken by someone standing on the crater floor, beside the rill he had noticed earlier. There were several large boulders in the foreground and he saw that one or two of them appeared to be speckled with something that glistened in the slanting sunlight. Similar veins of this whitish material were just visible along one inner edge of the rill itself.

Quite possibly, he thought, these were crystals of some mineral deposit, their faceted faces catching and reflecting the sunlight. On the other hand, there was just the chance they might be the source of the organism and —

He thought about this for a moment and then it hit him. Quite suddenly he forgot his weariness. Scraping back his chair quickly, he crossed to the communicator.

Brander's lined face appeared on the small screen a few moments later. The security chief said tiredly, 'If it's about that thermonuclear device, I'm trying to arrange a flier this very minute and — '

'I want you to cancel that order. It's important you don't drop that bomb.'

'You mean you don't want that area cauterized?' The other stared at him in amazement. 'But I thought that Doctor Corval — '

'I know what Doctor Corval said. But we overlooked one thing. We need a supply of living organisms if we're to have any chance of producing a satisfactory serum. That crater is the only known source on the planet. We have to get a sample first.'

'All right, I'll cancel the bomb and — ' Brander broke off as the implications behind Naysmith's second remark sank in. 'What do you mean you have to get a sample of living organisms. You can't mean that — '

'I want to go out to Lowell as soon as possible. I know all about your directive, but this is vital.'

'What? Do you know what you're asking? Two men have already died and — '

'I know all that. But there has to be some transport available on the base with automatic handling devices on board.'

'Well . . . I guess there is. I only hope you appreciate the risk you're taking.'

Naysmith ignored that. It was a risk.

Even in a suit and enclosed inside a vehicle, there was always the risk of contamination and infection. But there was no other course open to them. He was convinced of that.

'How long before such a vehicle can be made ready? This is imperative. And you'll have to lift Directive SB 17-5Z.'

There was a long pause. Then Brander said, 'I think I can lay on a vehicle for you in half an hour.'

'Good. I'll be ready by then. It's possible Doctor Corval will want to come too.'

'Then I'll leave you to arrange that with him.'

'All right. Just get that vehicle. We'll also need a driver if you can get one who's prepared to take a chance.'

'That may not be too easy. Everybody is scared right now. I'll see what I can do.'

'I don't care if you have to order one, coerce one, or even threaten one to take us there. Just do it.' Naysmith broke the connection and then called Corval.

The other looked as if he had just woken from a deep sleep. But he jerked awake as Naysmith explained the position to him. Then he said, with a trace of excitement: 'You're right, of course. We almost destroyed the only chance we have of making that serum. I'll meet you at the main airlock in half an hour.'

★ ★ ★

The huge metal doors of the hangar that housed the larger vehicles slid open slowly, revealing the gaunt landscape beyond as the harsh light from inside the dome spilled out into the night. There was little to be seen beyond the widening swathe of white brilliance. The sky was clear and starlit but the stark contrast between the light inside the dome and the blackness of the surrounding terrain was such that he could make out few details.

Naysmith was seated in the curved bucket seat on one side of the driver with the curved plastiglass of the observation port directly in front of him, giving him an almost one hundred and eighty degree panoramic view.

Corval sat some distance behind, close

to the small electronic board that operated the remote handling equipment. All three men wore protective suits as an additional safeguard against the hazard of infection.

The driver was a hawk-faced man in his late thirties, his features just visible behind the transparent mask. Naysmith wondered whether he had volunteered for this mission or been pressurised into it by Brander. Either way, they were here and ahead of them was — what?

Naysmith tried not to think of the danger they might encounter, concentrating his thoughts on the task that faced them. That was all that really mattered. Getting those samples back to base safely.

The broad track that had led across the sand and rock from the base towards the spaceport was scarcely visible now. The violent dust storm of the previous day had almost totally erased it and there was a foot-high ridge of sand on the lip of the massive airlock where it had been driven up against the base of the dome by the high wind.

Slowly, they commenced to move

forward, the flexible treads churned up little eddies of dust as they passed out of the dome and onto the surface.

'You reckon we'll find anything out at Lowell, Doctor?' The driver spoke harshly without turning his head. His hands were steady on the controls.

'That's something we won't know until we get there,' Corval said. 'How long do you figure it will take us?'

'Six, maybe seven hours,' answered the other. 'The terrain gets a little rough once we cross that low escarpment yonder.' He pointed with a gloved hand.

Turning his head a little, Naysmith made out the low ridge immediately ahead of them, perhaps a kilometre away. There was a deep vee-shaped notch in the rock and they were headed straight towards it.

Behind them the wide airlock had closed and they were now in almost total darkness except for a scattering of lights from the other domes and the beam of the forward searchlight playing on the rock formations ahead.

Naysmith shifted himself into a more

comfortable position in the hard seat. He felt clumsy in the protective suit. As they rolled forward he saw that the notch ahead was, indeed, a pass through the escarpment. As they entered the deep shadow he felt the nearness of the rising walls of sand-eroded stone on either side. There were so many similarities here to the terrain on the Moon with which he was familiar. Yet one still got the feeling that life existed on this planet. The science fiction writers of more than a century before had peopled Mars with long-dead cities that lay slumbering in red-rust deserts, relics of an age of intelligence that had died out while their own ancestors on Earth had lived in trees.

The true picture was vastly different. There had never been life on Mars. It was still a virgin world except for the mere handful of people who had come out from Earth and Luna. Whether it would ever have produced its own evolutionary scheme of indigenous beings was sheer speculation.

They rumbled through the narrow pass and came out into a thickly cratered region. Here they were forced to drive more slowly as the ground lifted and fell steeply with craters of all sizes looming up on either side. Once or twice they passed supply caches along the sinuous track, each marked with a brilliant red sign that thrust up stiffly out of the rock. Noticing them, Naysmith remembered the vast dust storms that frequently scoured the planet, blanketing whole regions for days, sometimes for weeks or months at a time. Such caches were essential in the event of an expedition losing themselves in such blinding storms.

He leaned back in his seat and tried to get his thoughts into some form of order. Once they reached Lowell they would have to work quickly and efficiently with each man knowing exactly what to do. There could be no mistakes.

The automatic probes were situated near the rear of the crawler. They were all operated by the controls along the small, square panel. Scoops would thrust themselves out through sealed gaskets, dig into the soil for samples, then drop them into the small containers outside the vehicle.

Drills and picks would chip away at the hard rock, taking samples and likewise storing them in the containers.

They could not risk bringing them inside even though they were all wearing protective suits. Not only was there the risk of exposing themselves to the infection but also of cross-contamination. All of these exterior containers had been thoroughly sterilised prior to leaving the base.

'Have you been to Lowell before?' Corval asked the driver.

The man shook his head. 'I've been on Mars for two years and on three expeditions, but I've never visited Lowell. Tell you the truth, I'm not sure I want to go there now.'

'You scared?' Naysmith asked.

'Too damn right I'm scared, doc. After what I've heard on the Base, who wouldn't be?'

'That's good.'

'It's good to be scared?'

'Yes. Because a man who's frightened doesn't take any unnecessary chances. And we don't want any heroics on this trip.'

'You won't get any from me, you can be sure of that. My orders were to take you there and to stay inside the crawler at all times. That's exactly what I'm going to do.'

'There's just one thing. Once we reach Lowell we'll have to go down onto the crater floor. Think you can manage to get this crawler down without any trouble?'

'Depends on what we find when we get there. Usually it's not easy to cross the ringwall of a crater. Unless you're lucky and find a break wide enough to take the crawler and the slope isn't too steep.'

Naysmith turned his attention to the terrain across which they were now travelling. Up ahead, a line of craters just showed along the horizon, their topmost peaks etched blackly against the stars. Although the crater walls were only a couple of hundred metres in height, they were still impressive. He recalled what Jordan had said about the frequency of these almost perfectly straight lines of craters.

Unless one assumed that a line of meteors had plunged down onto the

Martian surface within seconds of each other such formations could not have been formed by meteoric impact. The more feasible explanation was the result of vulcanism along some fault line in the Martian crust.

As they drove slowly around the towering walls he tried to make out the surfaces of the rocks in the probing searchlight beam. Had vulcanism played a major part in their formation one would have expected to see some sign of heat in these rocks; some smoothing of their surfaces such as would have been produced by an outflow of liquid magma. But as far as he was able to determine through the observation window, they looked little different from the majority of lunar rocks he had seen.

Shortly before midnight, with the terrain around them etched with long, knife-edged shadows, the driver pointed directly ahead.

'There it is,' he said quietly. 'Lowell.'

Naysmith half rose from his seat to get a better view. The crater was situated in a comparatively flat, smooth region of rock and dust. It still lay beyond the reach of the searchlight mounted on the front of the crawler and all he got was a vague impression of midnight black rock walls rising sheer from the plain. But even this impression was enough to show him there was something strange about this formation. Then he realised what it was.

During all the hours they had been working their way northward from Syrtis Base, he had been watching the numerous craters they passed, noticing the weathered smoothness where rock had been scoured by flying sand and dust over long millenia. Here, however, the walls that spiked up from the flat plain were sharp and ragged. There had been little, if any, weathering of the rock. It looked, for all the world, like a gigantic bubble on the surface of some thick, sticky liquid that had burst and been frozen just at the moment of bursting.

Corval had noticed this aspect too. He said: 'There's no doubt in my mind that your friend Jordan was right. It can't have been formed more than a little while ago compared with all the others we've seen.'

To the driver, Naysmith said: 'Is it possible to get this crawler down onto the crater floor?'

'We can try. It's been done with some of the other formations, but this doesn't look too easy.'

They edged their way forward. Long shadows appeared and then fled away as the searchlight beam touched the rising pinnacles of rock. Slowly, they circled the massive ringwall. A long, rubble-strewn slope surrounded much of the crater.

'Doesn't look too hopeful.' The driver's hands hovered over the controls. The engine whined shrilly as the tracks eased over the piles of rubble.

'Maybe that's the reason Gordon had to go down on foot,' Corval suggested.

'Let's hope not.' Naysmith tried to force enthusiasm into his tone. Inwardly, he was beginning to feel less optimistic about the outcome of this trip than he had when they left the base. There appeared to be no opening at all in the ringwall and much of it seemed virtually unclimbable even in the lower gravity of Mars.

He tried to call to mind the photographs he had seen taken from the orbiting satellites. Had they shown any crack in the ringwall where it might be possible to take the crawler through. He wished he had brought them with him to study.

The driver shifted into the lowest gear as a rocky mound appeared directly in front of him. Gently, he increased the power to the tracks. The crawler tilted precariously as the nose lifted. Rocks and boulders crumbled under the treads. Then they failed to maintain a grip on the treacherous surface. The crawler slid back and came to a stop.

'No good,' muttered the driver. 'We'll never get over that. I'll back off and see how far this ridge extends.'

Cautiously, he put the crawler into reverse, halted again when they were some thirty metres away. Deftly, he manipulated the controls of the searchlight, swinging the brilliant beam along the ridge that ran down from the outer ringwall into the darkness. They had already dimmed the lights inside the

152

vehicle to see better and some five minutes later they had their answer.

Disappointment tinged Naysmith's voice as he said flatly: 'That ridge must extend across the plain for more than a couple of kilometres. We'll have to make a detour around it.'

'Maybe not.' The driver leaned sideways in his seat, fumbled for a switch on his right.

'You know of some other way?' asked Corval.

'If that ridge isn't any more than a few metres thick we might be able to blast a way through it. These crawlers are equipped with laser cannons. There are a couple in a turret on top. They can be used to cut a way through solid rock provided it isn't too thick. They would be useless as far as the ringwall is concerned, but we might carve a way through that ridge.'

'Then try it,' urged Naysmith.

'I'll have to douse the searchlight otherwise we'll use too much power.' The driver snapped down a switch and there was pitch darkness outside except for the faint sheen of starlight. The ridge was just visible as a mound of blackness against the horizon, with the mighty rim of the ringwall to their left, blotting out much of the sky in that direction.

A few seconds later there was a faint, high-pitched hum and then twin beams of light speared towards the rock. The high intensity radiation hit the rock simultaneously. It began to melt and flow and Naysmith, shielding his eyes against the vicious glare, saw splinters of stone go flying in all directions.

'This may take a little time but it seems to be working,' the driver said. He spoke through tightly clenched teeth.

Naysmith sat back in his seat and forced himself to relax. The raw energy of the lasers was now beginning to chew its way through the barrier in a coruscating glare of light. The lasers had been aimed to start at the top of the ridge and they slowly began to work their way down rather like a man dismantling a wall brick by brick.

The driver sat back, looked round. 'Might as well have some coffee while we're waiting,' he said, grinning. 'The lasers are linked to a mini-computer we have on board. They'll continue automatically until they get near ground level.'

The coffee too, was prepared automatically and ready within seconds. Drinking it while still wearing the protective helmet provided no difficulty and Naysmith was used to such procedures during his long stay on Luna.

By the time they had finished he felt warmer inside and already the lasers had sliced through the impeding ridge to within a short distance of ground level, opening up a pathway through the rock some two metres wide.

'It's going to be a tight squeeze but we'll make it,' the driver said, starting the engine. He switched off the laser cannons and turned on the searchlight. The rocks still glowed faintly as they edged their way through them into more open terrain.

Still the sheer cliffs of the ringwall loomed high on their left apparently unbroken. Damn, Naysmith thought, running his gaze over them. If the crater wall was complete all the way around the floor they didn't have a chance in hell of getting the crawler down. He didn't relish the idea of imitating Gordon and going in on foot, but getting samples of the virus was absolutely essential and there appeared nothing else for it.

Then Corval clutched his shoulder tightly, leaning forward in his seat. The doctor said excitedly: 'What's that over there, about forty metres ahead?'

The driver adjusted the searchlight, swinging it to the left. There was a sloping pile of debris jutting out from the crater and a stretch of black, featureless shadow along the ringwall. It extended for perhaps twenty metres before the searchlight beam picked out gullies and rocks where the crater rim began once more.

The gap in the ringwall showed clearly as they drew alongside. It had evidently been formed where debris had been thrown out in one preferential direction, probably just ahead of the meteor impact that had formed the crater. Even so, the incline looked terrifyingly steep as they drew nearer.

'I guess we won't find anywhere else where we can get down onto the floor,' the driver muttered. 'Better strap yourself into your seats. This is going to be rough,'

Automatically, Naysmith adjusted the broad straps around his middle. There came a change in the strident note of the engine. It grew harsher and more high-pitched as the nose of the crawler lifted upward alarmingly. The treads clawed at the loose rubble and the vehicle began to shake and vibrate violently from side to side.

'We'll never make it,' said Corval hoarsely. He gripped the sides of his seat with a nervous, convulsive strength.

'You evidently don't know the capabilities of these crawlers, doctor,' replied the driver.

The searchlight beam bobbed and swayed across the rocks in front of them as they crawled up the slope towards the looming crater rim. Sitting tensed in his seat, Naysmith had the frightening vision of the tracks failing to maintain their grip, sending them plummeting out of control down the slope behind them. He realised now why those two men had gone down on foot.

Five minutes passed with an agonising slowness. Then, when it seemed they must surely topple backward, they reached the crater lip. There was a sudden lurch that threw them forward against the restraining straps. Naysmith felt his stomach come up in protest. The vehicle tilted sideways, then came onto an even keel.

The floor of Lowell lay spread out before them, bathed in the glare of the searchlight. He recognised it at once from the photographs in Jordan's report. The long ragged rill running diagonally across it showed clearly except where the shadow of the left hand wall fell across it.

'Now this is going to be somewhat more difficult,' called the driver. He sounded oddly unperturbed. 'There must be a forty-five degree slope down onto the crater floor. You still want to go through with this?'

'We've no other choice,' Corval said tightly. 'What are our chances?'

'Well, the crawler has a very low centre of gravity. We should be all right but I can't guarantee anything. I doubt if anyone has done this sort of thing before.'

'Then go ahead.'

They bumped forward across the wide rampart and approached the inner lip where the ground dropped away at a dizzying angle. In the pitch darkness they were forced to rely solely on the searchlight for any illumination.

Maybe it was better this way, thought Naysmith tautly. At least, it might alleviate in some small way the inevitable sense of vertigo. The sensation, when it came, was far from pleasant. Later, when he looked back on it, he described it to Carine Wilder as rather like falling in an elevator after the supporting cable had suddenly snapped.

Above the whine of the engine, they heard the grating rattle of the treads as they fought to keep their grip on the slippery, treacherous surface. There was the impression of rushing headlong into a bottomless abyss with no brakes, no means of halting that terrifying fall.

Once the treads did fail to hold and they slid out of control for what seemed an interminable period before the hard metal gripped once more and the savage, forward motion eased a little. Naysmith felt the sweat drip from his forehead into his eyes and he instinctively put up a gloved hand to wipe it away before realising that he was unable to do so. His stomach muscles tightened themselves into a hard painful knot, Had it been a smooth, bearable motion, he might not have felt quite so bad. But it was not. The crawler would seem to halt momentarily and then lunge forward like a maddened horse.

'We're almost there.' yelled the driver. 'Hang on.'

There was an abrupt sensation as if everything had fallen out of the bottom of the world. Then they had come to rest on an even keel. Naysmith felt the breath gush from his lips in a long soundless sigh of utter relief. It was a little difficult to believe they had made it and were still alive. He did not pause to think they would have to go through the same thing again on the return trip.

Carefully, the driver turned the crawler until the flooding beam of the searchlight bathed the ragged lip of the wide crack across the crater floor with an almost eye-searing brilliance.

'Let's hope you find what you're looking for,' he said tautly. 'I'd sure hate to think this trip had all been for nothing.'

'Don't worry,' Corval said. 'We both feel exactly the same way about it. Think you can edge forward so that we can take a couple of samples from just inside that crack.'

The mobile laboratory began to creep forward, a little way at a time, until it came to a grinding halt less than a couple of metres from the nearer lip of the rill.

'How far down do you reckon that crack goes?' asked the driver.

'We don't know,' Naysmith answered. 'It could be anything from a few metres to a kilometre or more.'

'I remember one of the scientists at the base saying he believed this crater to be hollow.'

Corval glanced up sharply. 'Why did he say that?'

'Something to do with a bulge in the middle of the crater floor and some seismological measurements he carried out. I don't think anyone took him seriously though.'

'If he was right it might explain a lot of things.' Naysmith felt a stir of excitement at the possibility. 'There could be a huge underground chamber down there probably caused by a bubble of high temperature gas. There may even have been water there too at one time.'

'So there would be all the ingredients necessary to form long-chain amino acids and perhaps life?' Corval sounded equally excited.

Naysmith shrugged. He pushed himself out of his seat. 'Perhaps. It's not beyond the bounds of possibility. But we're just speculating at the moment. We need the evidence of those samples before we can even begin to theorise.'

He picked his way carefully past masses of equipment to the rear of the crawler and lowered his body clumsily into the small bucket seat in front of the control panel. Corval squatted beside him and flicked down the switch that put on the rear floodlight.

'Can you make out anything?'

Naysmith pointed. 'Those whitish specks that sparkle in the light. I noticed them on the photographs taken by one of the earlier expeditions.'

'And you reckon they may have something to do with our organisms?'

'I'm not sure. But they're certainly the oddest thing I've ever seen. They look even more peculiar now that I can see them at first hand,'

In the brilliant glare of the floodlight it was easy to pick out the irregular patches and blobs that glittered on the surface of the greyish-black rock just below the rim of the wide crack. His first thought that they might have been some kind of crystalline deposit was clearly wrong. He had never seen a mineral that looked anything like this.

For one thing, they did not appear to be embedded in the rock as a crystalline material would have been. Nor were they arranged in any vein-like structure. Rather they were splotches of brilliant white clustered on the surface. Something like glistening patches of mucus or some of the bacterial colonies he had encountered numerous times in his career.

'Have you ever operated one of these remotely-controlled scoops before?' asked Corval.

Naysmith shook his head. 'Nothing quite like this. We normally used glove boxes for this purpose.'

He pushed the two buttons marked PROJECT SCOOP. There was a faint click, then the whirring of a concealed motor. Just beyond the viewing window he made out the telescopic arms extending towards the surface.

Two stubby levers that could be grasped in the palms clearly operated them. Each had a button at the top that, the driver explained, closed the scoops.

It took him a few moments to get used to handling the telescopic arms since not only was there a slight delay between operating the levers and the transmission of power to the arms, but it was not easy to coordinate the movements of lever and scoop.

Gradually, however, he became. accustomed to the various movements. Peering intently through the window, he edged the scoop along the rock, scraping small pieces of the whitish material away. It did not flake off as he had expected but seemed to possess a curiously rubber-like consistency that resisted the movement of the scoop. At length, however he succeeded in detaching a number of small samples.

'Now comes the tricky part,' he said, speaking more to himself than to Corval.

Gingerly, he retracted the tubular arms to half their former length. He could just make out the metal canisters projecting from the outside of the crawler. Leaning over, Corval touched the button that flipped the lids back and, after several attempts, Naysmith succeeded in depositing the samples inside. The lids were replaced and Naysmith sat back in the seat, letting his breath go in little pinches through his nostrils.

'That's that,' he said. 'Perhaps we'd better take a sample of the rock too while we're here. I'd hate to get back to base and find that we've been mistaken all the time and those patches aren't the organism after all.'

Ten minutes later, a small piece of rock had been chipped away and placed in one of the containers.

'So far, so good,' muttered Corval. 'What now?'

Switching off the power to the controls, Naysmith turned to the driver. 'We'll check a couple of those large boulders strewn around the floor.'

By the time they had completed their collection of samples it was almost dawn. In spite of all his work, the fact that he had been awake for almost twenty-four hours, and the knowledge that they still had to make their way back to Syrtis Base, Naysmith was scarcely able to restrain his excitement.

Taking their places in the nose of the crawler, they strapped themselves in securely. The engine started with a throbbing roar, feeding power to the tracks. Outside, the sky was brightening with a pinkish-violet flush, touching the underside of the few hazy clouds. A few dust eddies whirled and chased themselves across the crater floor as they began to move towards the distant rim.

'Wind's getting up.' commented the driver. There was a note of unease in his voice. 'Could be there's a dust storm on the way.'

'Let's hope we can stay clear of it until we reach base.' Corval leaned back in his seat and surrendered himself to the deep-seated weariness in his body.

Naysmith said nothing. He was eyeing the steep incline that led up to the crater rim where the wide opening through which they had earlier come now showed clearly in the brightening dawn. Now that it was possible to see it clearly, it looked even more impassable than before. For a moment, he doubted the ability of the crawler to haul them all the way to the top.

They reached the bottom of the ascent and started up, moving painfully slowly, with the engine shrieking shrilly. The side-to-side rocking motion of the vehicle became more violent as they crunched over rows of upthrusting boulders that lay in their path.

The sun came up behind them, illuminating the inner ringwall with a flood of light, making every little crack and crevice stand out through the bulbous window. Beside him, the driver applied more power to the treads but their forward movement increased only marginally.

We're like a fly crawling up a wall, Naysmith thought, only we're not really as adaptable to such travel. It won't take much to send us hurtling back onto the crater floor and —

His thoughts gelled at a sudden shout from Corval. Momentarily, he turned his head to look at the doctor, then whirled back to stare in the direction of the other's pointing finger. There had been a look of astonished terror frozen onto Corval's features but at first he could not make out what the other had seen.

Then he lifted his gaze and felt his mouth go suddenly dry, felt his heart jump, hammering, into his throat. It was impossible to tell what had caused the huge boulder, poised on the crater rim, to move. It could have been some delayed effect of the laser blasts that had opened a way through the narrow ride; a weakness

168

in the ringwall that had been enhanced by their rumbling passage down the inner slope. Or it might just have been sheer misfortune that it happened when it did.

The boulder seemed to move in slow motion although in reality was gathering momentum rapidly. Through startled eyes, Naysmith watched it leap high into the air as it struck an impeding rock. It smashed onto the wide track made by the crawler's treads a few hours earlier and came hurtling towards them.

The driver yelled something that Naysmith couldn't make out above the grinding roar of the engine as he tried to slew the crawler out of the path of the onrushing mass of rock. But the warning had come far too late. Their forward momentum was much too slow to give any chance of manoeuvre.

Naysmith had time for the stunned realisation that they were going to be hit. Then the boulder crashed into the side of the crawler. There was a moment of utter chaos, of toppling perspective and then everything went dark.

7

By all the rules, the crawler should have been wrecked beyond repair, the atmosphere inside should have dissipated into the thinner Martian atmosphere, and the three men killed outright. That none of this happened was little short of miraculous, a combination of circumstances which represented a million to one chance against their occurrence.

Naysmith should have lost consciousness when the tremendous impact snapped the safety straps and threw him sideways from his seat, hurling him savagely against the inner shell of the crawler. He was almost unconscious, but not quite. There was a mindless period during which events seemed to be happening outside of himself and in which he had no part. There were noises but he could not fix upon their origin, rays of light that swirled about him like the sound, confused and non-directional.

Ages later, it seemed, there came the moment of returning sensibility. He was lying awkwardly on the canted floor of the crawler, his legs twisted under him and a heavy weight lying against his right side. The sound he had been aware of resolved itself into the roar of the engine, still hammering away in the eternal stillness of Mars. There was also a fainter, closer sound; a continual hiss next to his ear, which he recognised as the air-cycling unit of his suit, still functioning in spite of what had happened.

He groaned and tried to push himself upright. Twisting his head around he found the driver lying hard against him. The man was still unconscious, but came round as Naysmith moved him gently. In the rear of the crawler, Corval was sprawled on the floor, arms outflung.

Naysmith pulled in a deep breath. It steadied him and enabled his thoughts to form more clearly. He recalled the huge bulk of the boulder bounding down the slope towards the crawler and the shattering crash of the impact. But how long ago had that been — and more important, how much damage had they sustained? If the crawler was out of commission, then they might have to stay there forever — or at least until Brander decided that something had gone wrong and sent another vehicle to look for them.

He wondered briefly whether Brander would even consider that alternative. Maybe the security chief had been pushed so close to the point of a breakdown that he would consider there was nothing more that could be done in the time available and he would activate those nuclear devices.

The thought sent a shiver through him and then reason prevailed. That was something Brander couldn't do, he realised suddenly. Because one of the three men who had to feed those impulses into the central computer was lying on the crawler floor only a few feet away from him.

The driver groaned and tried to pull himself into his seat, then stopped as he realised it was no longer upright.

'What in hell happened?' he mumbled, holding onto the metal side for support. There was an ugly purple bruise on the side of his jaw where he must have struck his head on the inside of the helmet. He rubbed his side experimentally and winced.

'That boulder which was dislodged from the rim of the crater. Must've hit the crawler a godalmighty wallop.'

Awkwardly, the driver stumbled to his feet. 'Better check the air. How long have we been out?'

Naysmith glanced at his watch. Miraculously it was still going.

'Nearly a couple of hours.'

Flipping down a row of switches with stiff fingers, the other shut off the roaring engine. Then he checked the air pressure, gave a satisfied nod. 'Looks all right. If there are any leaks in the hull they can't be serious otherwise we would have lost most of the air by now. Pressure's equalised pretty quickly on Mars.'

A movement behind him made Naysmith turn his head quickly. Corval was sitting on the crawler floor shaking his head numbly.

'You all right?' Naysmith asked, helping him to his feet.

'I think so. Last thing I remember is

that rock hitting the side of the crawler. I figured it really would be the last thing I'd see.'

'We've been bloody lucky,' muttered the driver, turning from the controls. 'By rights, we should have been crushed.'

'At least the engine is still working.'

'Maybe so, but it'll be a goddamn miracle if we get out of here. There must have been some damage caused. You don't get hit by a couple of dozen tons of solid rock and come out of it unscathed.'

Naysmith thought about the samples in those metal canisters hanging outside the rear of the crawler. Somehow, they had to get them back to base whatever the cost.

He said thinly, 'Do you reckon we can make it back to base if we get this crawler back on the level?'

'Depends. We'll have to check out the external damage first and that means going outside,'

The implications behind the driver's remark were not lost on Naysmith. From the start of this mission it had been considered imperative that no one should leave the comparative safety of the crawler. All the evidence they had so far was that so long as one remained inside the vehicle while in the vicinity of Lowell, the risk of contracting the disease was negligible.

Even though they had only two cases to go on, the chance of getting it by going out onto the crater floor was almost one hundred per cent certain.

'Let's take a look at what we can see through the observation viewers first,' Corval suggested. 'There's no point in going outside until we know what we're up against.'

The forward observation port was sufficiently bulbous to extend beyond the sides of the hull and Naysmith pressed his helmet hard against the plastiglass in an attempt to see along the crawler.

As far as he could estimate, the crawler was tilted at an angle of about twenty degrees with the treads sticking up from the friable crater floor. A thick film of greyish-white dust streaked with red covered the entire side of the vehicle.

'There doesn't seem to be much damage this side,' he said, turning to

175

where Corval was peering along the other part of the hull.

'The tracks seem to be stuck into the dust layer on this side.'

'Any sign of damage?'

'We seem to have lost the forward searchlight unit. Looks as though it's been sheared off.'

'If that's the full extent of the damage we ought to make it.' Naysmith glanced towards the driver who was still checking the controls, his body jammed across the seat. 'How much fuel do we have? Enough to get us back to base?'

'Sure. And then some. These crawlers are equipped to drive a couple of hundred kilometres without refuelling. No problem there.'

'Then let's try to get this thing onto an even keel.'

'How do you propose we do that without going outside?' Corval asked.

'Maybe if we shifted ourselves and all the portable equipment over to one side the excess weight might be enough to tilt it. As far as I can see there's nothing stopping it.'

'It's worth a try,' the driver acknowledged. 'To be honest, I didn't relish the thought of going outside. Not after what happened to the others.'

Naysmith could understand his reasons. One didn't deliberately commit suicide in such a way. Together, they pulled and hauled all of the moveable equipment from one side of the crawler to the other. In the confined space it was not easy and the task was made even more difficult by the angle of the floor.

'She's moving!'

Naysmith felt the shuddering beneath his feet as Corval yelled the warning. There was a grating wrench that shivered throughout the entire length of the crawler. Desperately he hung onto one of the metal supports, felt the jar hammer through his legs as the crawler toppled back onto an even keel. He was sweating profusely inside the heavy suit.

Outside, the cloud of pink dust subsided slowly as the driver edged his way forward and sank gratefully into his seat. He peered through the observation window for a moment, cast a quick glance towards the rim of the crater that towered high against the pink-purple heavens, then thumbed the stud that started the engine. There was a coughing thump and then the motor came on with its full-throated roar. Deftly, the driver engaged gear.

A deep shudder vibrated through the crawler but nothing else happened. The air outside filled again with churned dust clouds but there was no movement.

For a moment, the driver applied more power to the engine, then eased back on the throttle and disengaged the gear.

'It's no use. The treads must have been damaged. Probably one or more connecting links broken.'

'Can it be repaired?'

'Oh, sure. We carry spare links and treads.' The driver's tone was dry. 'But it means we'll have to go outside.'

Naysmith hesitated. He knew, perhaps more than either of the other men, the risk they would run if they left the crawler. He tried to think of any other alternative but apart from waiting there until rescue came from Syrtis Base — if it ever did come — he could think of nothing.

'Well?' said the driver.

He reached a sudden decision. It was probably the wrong one, he told himself, and it went against everything he believed. 'All right. I'll go outside. What about you two?'

He saw the hesitation mirrored on their faces. He didn't really have the right to ask them to do this, but he knew he would never be able to repair the treads himself.

'All right.' The driver nodded and eased himself out of his seat. 'If I'm to get this disease it might as well be here as inside the base.'

Corval made to speak but Naysmith cut him off. 'I think you'd better stay on board. We can manage this between us and just in case the worst does happen, we'll need one of us to carry through the rest of the experiments. No sense in risking both our lives.'

Corval was obviously relieved but he made no comment as the driver went aft for the repair tools.

Two minutes later, Naysmith was standing beside the driver on the floor of Lowell. The sun was high now, throwing black shadows across the boulder-strewn floor. Carefully, they made their way around the vehicle, checking the tracks and it was as they reached the rear that they saw the fresh danger that had lurked, unsuspected, in store for them.

The miraculous sequence of events following on from the fall of the boulder, and which had undoubtedly saved them from destruction, had posed a fresh problem in its wake. It was the driver who saw it first. He halted abruptly in his tracks and Naysmith, following close behind, collided with him, almost knocking him to the ground.

'My God, will you look at that!'

Naysmith turned his gaze in the direction of the other's pointing finger.

The huge boulder which he had expected to see somewhere on the crater floor was not there. Where it might have been was a gaping hole some thirty metres wide with steep-sided edges that vanished precipitously into the stygian blackness below the crater.

In its own way, the shock to Naysmith's nervous system was as severe as the sight of seeing that boulder careening down the slope towards them had been. He stood stock still while his mind tried to take in what had happened. Only slowly, did he manage to piece together a probable sequence of events that explained why they had not been obliterated by the impact of those tons of rock.

Somehow, the massive boulder must have hit an obstruction just before it reached the crawler and its forward momentum had been sufficient to lift it clear of the slope so that it had caught the searchlight unit on top of the crawler as it had bounced over them.

What had followed next he could only imagine but it seemed that the boulder must have struck the crater floor like a small meteorite.

Had it happened virtually anywhere else on the surface it would merely have embedded itself deep in the sand and rock. But there had been an underground bubble of high-pressure gas just below the surface at the point, a bubble that had slowly been working its way up from the depths ever since Lowell had first been formed.

The shattering impact had fractured the unstable rock immediately above it, releasing the gas in a wide jet and opening up the chasm that now confronted them. Perhaps, Naysmith thought, if it had not been for this high-pressure gas, striking the side of the crawler like a jet of liquid, the vehicle would have slipped back into that gaping hole and it would have been the end of them.

As it was, the crawler was balanced precariously on the lip of the chasm and It was going to be a very tricky exercise trying to manoeuvre the crawler away from the crumbling rock once they had carried out the necessary repairs.

The driver had realised this too for he stepped back a couple of paces, watching his footing, and surveyed the situation. He said harshly, 'That bloody hole must be two or three hundred metres deep. If we fall back into that we'll never claw our way out.'

'Let's tackle first things first. The tracks seem okay this side.'

They worked their way slowly around the rear of the crawler.

On the way, Naysmith noticed that the metal canisters containing the shiny material, were still intact. It was not until he was at the other side examining the broken linkage in the treads that he realised what had been nagging at his mind for the past ten minutes. If there had been a gas bubble just beneath the surface — and those whitish deposits were the source of this virus, then the jet of high-pressure gas would have sprayed the entire crater with this organism.

He tried not to think about the inevitable consequences of that over the ensuing minutes as he fumblingly helped the driver replace the twisted linkages with new ones. His fingers moved automatically as he followed the directions given to him by his companion, tugging the bent pieces of metal free and inserting new ones.

'There,' The pilot stepped back, 'I figure that ought to hold until we get back to base. How are you feeling, doc?'

'Bloody hot.' In spite of the chill of the Martian day, it was unbearably warm inside the suit and his air was beginning to foul up. His tanks must be on the point of exhaustion.

The driver took his arm. He pointed. 'We'd better try to get started. I don't like the look of that sky up there.'

To the south the sky, which had been a pale mauve when they had first started work on the treads, was now a deeper, angry red and even through the helmet, Naysmith could make out a rising wail of sound.

'Dust storm?' he said as they stumbled around the crawler.

'You can bet on it. I've seen three while I've been out on the surface and in one and believe me it isn't an experience I want to go through again if I can avoid it.'

Naysmith climbed stiffly through the airlock, felt the other crush in beside him. Then the scene outside was blotted out as the exterior door slid shut. Pressures equalised within seconds and they stepped inside.

Corval glanced up questioningly as the pilot went quickly across to his seat.

'Better strap down,' Naysmith told him. 'There's a dust storm heading this way.'

What else can be against us as far as this investigation is concerned? Naysmith wondered dully as he sank down into his seat after clipping on a couple of fresh air supply tanks. It was as if Fate was deliberately conspiring to prevent them from saving the Base; as if the planet itself were determined to be rid of the intruders.

The engine started. The driver let it idle for several seconds listening intently to the throbbing beat until certain it was performing smoothly. Once they started to move forward there could be no mistakes, no faltering on the part of the main drive. There was that gaping hole immediately behind them and already the shuddering vibration of the crawler might be breaking down the rocky ledge on which they were poised.

'Ready?' the driver called.

'Let's go,' Naysmith replied. He felt tensed and knotted inside and no matter how hard he tried it was impossible for him to relax.

Carefully, the driver engaged the forward gear. Slowly, an inch at a time, they began to move. There was a hideous, frightening moment when the crawler lurched violently, threatened to slip backward. Naysmith's heart thudded with adrenalin-pumped fear. Then the vehicle steadied. They began to pull away. Turning his head, Naysmith caught a glimpse through the rear viewing port of the crater floor slipping away, the mouth of the gaping hole growing smaller with every second as they began their ascent towards the rim.

It seemed to take an eternity of sweating and mentally praying before they finally reached the narrow ledge that formed the inner lip of the massive ringwall. Now, he thought, we're comparatively safe. There's only the descent of the outer ringwall and then the trail back to Base.

Then his forehead prickled icily as he saw the wide, spreading curtain that had descended across the plain below them, a wavering wall of dust, which in places was so thick that no details could be seen through it.

'It's going to be a bad one,' the driver yelled above the roar of the engine. 'I'll try to get down onto the trail as quickly as I can. It's possible we may have to shelter in one of the ravines. I doubt if there's any chance of outrunning it.'

Naysmith nodded in acquiescence. He remembered how the dust storm of a couple of nights earlier had scoured the outside of the dome. Out here in the open it could be a hundred times worse. Those millions of whirling sand grains could easily work their way into the treads of the crawler and even though they would not stop the vehicle the driving wind could build up drifts sufficiently deep to bog them down.

A quarter of an hour later, on more level ground, with Lowell just visible on the skyline behind them, the storm closed in around them in earnest. The wind shrieked like a banshee around the hull. Surging columns of pink grains rattled and abraded the plastiglass.

Visibility dropped quickly until they were crawling forward in a dense mist that allowed them no glimpse at all of what lay about them.

Only the radar pulses, bouncing back from the solid objects in their path, provided a picture of the trail ahead. The driver's face was drawn into a permanent frown as he followed the trail marked out in glowing green lines on the small circular scope in front of him.

'I'm counting on reaching that narrow ravine about a kilometre ahead,' he said suddenly, breaking the long silence. 'We'll have to hole up there for a while until this storm blows itself out.'

'Why do that?' asked Corval. 'Surely we can navigate by the radar?'

'Sure,' agreed the other, 'but there's bound to be drifting in this wind and the radar won't show that up. If we plough straight into a ten-metre high drift, we're stuck until we dig ourselves out. That boulder also took away much of the laser cannon mounting. We can't use that.'

Naysmith's gaze focussed on the radarscope, trying to make sense out of the glowing green masses. There was undoubtedly a picture there but it was one he could not read clearly. No doubt the driver was able to correlate what he saw there with what was actually outside, but the thought did little to ease the tension in him.

The sound of the engine altered abruptly, rose shrilly in pitch. They slewed sideways and for a sickening moment Naysmith thought they were spinning aimlessly around, out of control.

The nose of the crawler lifted sharply, hung poised for a moment as if suspended in mid-air, then crashed down again with a jar that shook his whole body.

'We're already running into drifts,' yelled the driver as he wrestled savagely with the controls. 'Hang on. It's going to get a lot rougher before we reach that ravine.'

For close on twenty minutes they lurched and bumped through the swirling storm, their faces a ghastly hue in the deep pink light which suffused through the port. The sun was up there somewhere but it had vanished completely behind the sand curtain.

Then, almost as suddenly as it had begun, the wind dropped. The savage buffeting ceased. The crawler slowed, then slithered to a grinding halt. There was still very little light outside but the sand no longer swirled thickly around them and they were able to make out details of the nearer landscape. Tall, towering rock walls rose sheer on either side with looming, time-eroded crags overhanging the narrow trail.

Naysmith exhaled slowly and shifted his body into a more comfortable position. The far end of the ravine was just visible but beyond it was nothing. Only a short distance away, in front and behind them, the dust storm raged on but here in this sheltered haven, everything seemed quiet.

'I'll make us some coffee.' Naysmith got up and went to the rear of the crawler.

There was no telling how long they would have to remain in the ravine. He had virtually no first-hand experience of conditions on Mars but from what he knew, these storms were quite unpredictable both in their onset and duration. Some lasted for only a few hours before blowing themselves out while others continued for days on end with no let up in their savage fury.

We're on an alien planet, he thought, as he brewed the coffee in the special containers; one which we may never conquer completely. At the moment, all we can do is adapt and try our best to survive.

An hour passed, then two without any change in the dimness outside. Then, slowly, the haziness began to thin out. They could see a short distance beyond the far mouth of the ravine, then a little further.

The driver stirred in his seat. 'It seems to be thinning out. Reckon we'll be on our way again soon.'

'Thank God for that.' Corval rubbed his left shoulder. 'I was beginning to think we were stuck here for ever.'

Fifteen minutes later they rumbled out of the ravine, heading almost due south. Behind them, the departing fringes of the storm hazed the late afternoon sky while up ahead, the red sun was sinking rapidly towards the saw-toothed horizon.

'Another six hours and we should be back at base,' said the driver laconically. 'If you want to grab yourselves a few hours' sleep this is maybe the best chance you'll get. Everything should be plain sailing from here.'

Naysmith nodded slowly although whether the other was aware of his acquiescence it was impossible to tell. The man's eyes were fixed on the scene ahead in the fading sunlight.

Within the bulky protective suit it was not easy to relax or find a comfortable position. Naysmith eased himself around in the bucket seat for several moments, leaning his head back against the rest. After a while, he was able to relax a little, stretching his legs out as far as they would go in the confined space. A tiny, niggling voice at the back of his mind warned him it might be dangerous to relax too much but the idea seemed meaningless. His body ached in a dozen different places, a combination of the bruising it had received when they had been hit by that boulder and the unaccustomed work outside repairing the treads.

Sleep is all that matters, he thought. Peace of mind would be nice too but that would have to wait until they had this disease licked. He felt a stir of uneasy fear at that last thought. There was a dull tightness at the back of his eyes that seemed more intense now that he allowed his mind to dwell on it.

He recalled those intense headaches the two victims had complained of shortly before their bizarre deaths and his flesh was suddenly icily chill. Was this the beginning of such a symptom? Or just a natural reaction from staring too long into that blinding dust storm?

* * *

He woke, suddenly, to pale green dimness. For a moment he was lost, disorientated, his mind trying to determine where he vas. Then memory flooded back into his mind and he jerked upright in his seat. Sleep, the little death, had really taken a hold on him, he realised.

The powerful engine of the crawler was still throbbing in his ears so he knew they were still travelling across the crater-strewn desert. Outside, it was pitch black with nothing showing. He leaned forward and tried to see through the pale green reflection of the interior lights.

At first, he was aware only of the darker masses of the tall pinnacles of rocks and squat boulders against the slightly brighter starshine in the Martian heavens. Then he peered more closely, shading the plastiglass with his gloved hand. There was a faint twinkle of lights far in the distance like a tiny constellation of grounded stars.

As he leaned back, the driver said quietly. 'That's right, doc. Syrtis Base. I figure we're about a kilometre away.'

Now they were almost there, Naysmith found his mind leaping ahead. There were problems to be faced once they arrived. The three of them and the crawler would have to be quarantined, particularly the driver and himself. Yet in spite of this they would have to continue their work preparing a serum and working with this organism.

He turned over the various possibilities in his mind. The only feasible solution appeared to isolate the entire Pathology Department, remove Carine and the technicians until this was all over.

Less than an hour later they passed inside the huge airlock of the nearest dome, waited until it had closed behind them and the air pressures had equalised, then clambered awkwardly from the crawler.

With fumbling fingers, Naysmith pulled off his suit and drew in a deep breath of cool air. Beside him, the driver and Corval did likewise.

A moment later the communicator set high on the nearby wall erupted into life and Brander's harsh voice said: 'Everything all right, Doctor Naysmith?'

'We got the samples without any trouble but we have a problem.'

'What kind of problem?'

Naysmith licked his lips. 'A contamination problem, Brander. It's one we'll have to sort out here and now.'

'I don't understand.' There was a trace of puzzlement in the metallic voice.

'We hit trouble inside Lowell. The crawler was disabled by a boulder and I had to go outside to help repair the damage.'

'You what!' There was a pause then: 'I understood one of the conditions attached to this mission was that no one would go outside, no matter what.'

'Damn it all, there was nothing else to be done. It was either that or sit there and wait for a rescue mission that might never come. Do you think I wanted to step outside knowing what I do about this virus?'

There was a longer pause this time. Naysmith could visualise the security chief trying to get a grip on himself, trying to master one more pressure that was being put on him. Finally: 'All right, so you had to go out. Where does that leave us? We can't allow you back into the main section of the base. You realize that.'

'I also realise that I have a lot of work to do if this base is going to survive at all,' Naysmith retorted, biting down the anger he felt. Maybe going out of the crawler had been a crazy, indulgent flirtation with death — but as he saw it, it had also been absolutely necessary.

'All right,' Brander said, 'I'm prepared to listen to any ideas you may have. What do you suggest?'

'As far as I see it, there's only one course of action open to us. You know the layout of the base better than I do. Is there any way we can close off the entire Pathology Department so we can work in there without any risk of contaminating the rest of the Base?'

There was another uncomfortable silence while Brander turned the idea over in his mind. Naysmith turned towards Corval. Softly, he said: 'You don't have to be in on this if you don't want to.'

The other did not hesitate. He grinned. 'You know you'll never manage it without my help. I'm game.'

'Thanks.'

The communicator crackled loudly as Brander said: 'I've checked the layout of that dome, Naysmith. It might just be possible to do as you suggest. But it will

197

take a little time. We'll have to move everyone out and set up temporary airlocks along the corridors. Give me a couple of hours.'

Two more hours, Naysmith thought wearily. Two more lost out of the seventy-two which the security chief had given him before he put into operation the directive which would destroy the entire base and everyone in it.

8

The electron microscope confirmed everything they had half-expected and hoped
for. It also added a few further details that
were both puzzling and unexpected. The
whitish material was rather like a sponge.
This had first shown up on the conventional light microscope where it was possible
to use a much lower magnification to show
the overall gross structure. There, they
had found the spongy mass to possess a
cellular appearance.

Under the scanning electron microscope
the individual cells were literally teeming
with the wire-like organisms they had discovered earlier around the damaged optic
nerve.

'There can't be any doubt now,'
affirmed Corval. He straightened back in
his chair. Grinning wearily, he went on.
'Now that we have something to work
on I'll get a sample of that stuff and make
a serum. I'll have to use conventional

methods and hope they work — heat treatment in suspension, ultraviolet radiation, possibly followed by precipitation with an electrolyte.'

'How long will it take?'

'Hard to say. With the equipment we have here, I may be able to get something in a couple of hours.'

Naysmith nodded and punched the button that transferred one of the containers through the far wall and into the adjoining laboratory. Theoretically, if they injected a patient with a sterile suspension of the dead virus, the body stimulated the production of antibodies against the disease.

There were, of course, other methods, mainly useful in the case of bacteria such as inoculating a series of test animals with the living culture. During this process, the pathological agent became attenuated. Its virulence was reduced in a stepwise manner so that the final solution produced either a very slight reaction in a human being or no symptoms at all yet still imparting an active immunity to the disease.

On the base, however, they had only

the Black Norway rats and it seemed likely they might not give the desired effect although they still had them as a backup if, for any reason, their first attempt failed.

The one big problem, as he saw it, was that with such an alien organism as this, the human body might not produce the necessary antibodies. He did not dare consider the outcome if that should prove to be the case.

Sitting forward in his chair, he stared intently at the image on the screen, at the multitude of strand-like organisms that clustered thickly within the pores of the spongy material.

The next thing he knew was a light touch on his shoulder. With a start, he jerked upright, turned quickly. Carine stood beside him, a worried look on her face.

'What the devil are you doing here?' He spoke more harshly than he had intended. 'I gave orders that everyone was to be evacuated from this area of the dome.'

'I know. But I'm in this as much as you are.' There was a determined thrust to her chin. 'I'm staying.'

'I suppose you realise the risk you're taking. You know I had to go outside the crawler while we were inside Lowell.'

'So Brander told me.'

'Then — '

'Have you had a headache since leaving the crater?'

'Well, no. But that doesn't — '

'It's more than twenty hours since you left Lowell. Both of those men who died complained of such symptoms within a couple of hours of going into that crater.'

That's true, Naysmith thought. It was something he had not considered. It was no certain proof that he had not contracted the disease but at least it was something in his favour. He tried to derive some reassurance from the thought.

Instinctively, he glanced at his watch. It was almost 07.25. He had been asleep in front of the microscope for almost an hour.

Rubbing his eyes, he said. 'Reckon I must have dozed off.'

'You really ought to get some sleep. You've been on the go for more than forty hours.'

He got up and stretched his legs. He felt stiff and sore. 'I got a few hours on the crawler coming back.' Kneading the muscles at the back of his neck, he forced a smile. 'I'll be all right now.'

'We're all being pushed to the limit. Do you really think Brander will put that directive into operation if we fail to come up with the answer in time?'

'With those politicians floating around in orbit out there, I don't see he has any choice.'

'I suppose I never thought, until now, that it might end like this.'

'Scared?'

She nodded slowly, full lips pressed into a tight line. 'I can understand the fundamental reasoning behind it, but it still seems to be utterly pointless, destroying everything like that.'

'We're not finished yet.' He tried to force conviction into his tone. 'At least we got samples of that virus from Lowell. If we can only make a satisfactory serum, we have the answer.'

Once again, as he spoke, he had the unshakeable feeling they were missing something obvious. He tried to dig it out of the back of his mind and bring the elusive little thought out into the open, but it had tantalised him for only a moment. Now it was gone, Sighing, he gave up the attempt. Maybe it wasn't so important, after all.

Otherwise, he told himself, it would have stuck in his memory.

Corval came into the laboratory some fifteen minutes later. He looked utterly exhausted and dishevelled. In one hand he held a small tube closed with a rubber septum.

'That the serum?'

Corval held up the tube. 'This is it. I doubt if there can be any spore formation but just to be on the safe side I took it up to eighty degrees Centigrade three times over a period of two hours.'

He looked at Carine, then inquiringly at Naysmith.

'She insisted on joining us,' Naysmith said.

'That was a stupid thing to do.' There was no malice, only concern in the doctor's tone. He laid the serum on the bench and knuckled his eyes.

'We'll try it on those three in the

Experimental Laboratory,' Naysmith said, picking it up and examining it.

Corval rubbed a sleeve across his forehead. He gave a tired nod.

'Ordinarily I'd have preferred to test it on the rats first. We won't know whether or not it has any serious side effects. But with this threat of total extinction hanging over our heads there isn't time for that. Somehow, I don't think we have anything to lose giving it to those men.'

★ ★ ★

Standing in front of the wide impervious partition, Naysmith vas able to see the three patients through one of the small windows. None of them showed any sign of movement.

'How long have they been like this?' Corval turned to Carine.

'About five hours.'

'I see you've managed to rig up monitoring devices on all three. That'll be a big help.'

Carine nodded and pointed towards

the square console in the corner of the laboratory. 'We're recording their respiration, heartbeats and other bodily functions, all through the computer. There's also a multi-channel electroencephalograph making continuous recordings.'

'Excellent.'

Naysmith walked across to the console, watched the yellow-green traces on the bank of oscilliscopes.

'The alpha rhythms seem to be diagnostic of sleep,' he said finally.

'That ought to help things as well,' Corval nodded. 'Now we just have to decide whether to give all three massive doses of the serum or try to carry out a control experiment.'

Naysmith reached a decision. 'Give the serum to two of them and save the third as a control. We can always give him the serum if the others show any significant improvement. The fact they've lived so long under restraint indicates that the course of the disease isn't as rapid as we thought at first.'

'Right. Then we'll get started.' He handed the glass container to Carine together with a sterile hypodermic. 'Run these into that other room, please.'

A little while later the hypodermic and container came moving slowly along the narrow conveyor beyond the partition. Using the remotely-controlled mechanical hands, Corval positioned them in front of him, manipulating them deftly and delicately. It was clear he had used this technique several times before and was thoroughly familiar with it.

'How are you going to make the injection?' Naysmith asked.

'It won't be too difficult. I'll inject into the base of the neck. That's about the only suitable place which is exposed.'

Naysmith's heart was thudding steadily as he watched. In spite of Corval's experience it took several minutes before he was able to make the injections, depressing the plunger slowly. One of the two men stirred immediately after the slender needle was withdrawn, then relaxed. After swabbing the areas with alcohol, Corval motioned to Carine to remove the container and hypodermics.

'Now all we can do is wait. It'll be

some time before we know if the serum is successful,'

'How long do you reckon it will be before we know anything definite, one way or the other?' Carine asked.

'I only wish I knew. I've the feeling we're still working in the dark. At least, now you've set up these monitors, they may tell us something soon.'

Naysmith gave one last glance through the small window. The three men lay close together on their sides, quiet and unmoving. From where he stood, they might have been dead.

* * *

In the small canteen adjoining the laboratory, Naysmith punched himself a cup of coffee and sipped it slowly. Curiously, he didn't feel hungry although it was more than a day since he had eaten anything substantial. Usually the canteen was crowded with technicians but now, with this entire wing blocked off by the hastily-erected airlocks, it was empty apart from themselves.

Leaning back in his chair, he flexed his shoulder muscles and tried to ease the ache in them. Corval stretched and relaxed also.

Carine brought her coffee across and sank down in the chair next to Naysmith. For a moment, she leaned against him, purposefully and the faint scent she used touched his nostrils.

There was a deep weariness in her brown eyes as she smiled at him and he felt a sudden compassionate warmth burst inside him.

Perhaps when all this is finished and there's no longer the press of time crushing us and controlling our every action, he thought, there might be time to relax and get to know each other better. He had felt strangely attracted to her when they had first met and he had the idea this feeling was reciprocated. But this was neither the time nor the place for anything like that.

Across the table, Corval said quietly. 'I think this is as good an opportunity as any to go over all we know about this organism and the Lowell Syndrome.

There may be some vital clue we've missed.'

Naysmith set down his cup and rested his weight on his elbows.

'Well, we know that it can somehow penetrate a normal spacesuit, possibly because of its overall dimensions. That means there's very little we can do physically to protect ourselves. And we also know that it exists, as far as we can tell, only in one particular location.'

'Doesn't that strike you as odd?' Carine put in. 'Even if that crater is only a few years old and even if this organism was brought to Mars by some meteorite, it should have spread long before now.'

'Quite right,' Corval said. 'Wind currents alone would carry it an appreciable distance across the terrain in a very short time.'

'I've been thinking about that,' Naysmith said. 'There seems to be only one explanation for that. Some form of symbiosis with that spongy material. It may even be its natural host.'

'That seems a logical assumption,' Corval agreed after a brief pause. 'So we

210

still have the means of destroying the source if not entirely eliminating it from the base.'

'That's right.' Naysmith felt some of his tension begin to return. 'It's inside the base.'

'So what else do we know?' Carine stared down into her coffee as if hoping to find the answer there.

'We know that the major symptom is an extremely powerful hallucination which makes the victim believe that environmental conditions are somehow reversed. He thinks he's out on the planetary surface when he's really safe inside a vehicle or in the base. And if we can restrain the patient so that he doesn't die of asphyxiation, the disease isn't fatal. At least, not in the short term.'

'There's also the likelihood that certain people possess some form of immunity to the disease.' Corval swallowed a couple of amphetamine tablets, grimacing a little. 'Of that first expedition, one man went into Lowell on foot, and he contracted the disease. The situation repeated itself with the second team. None of the other

211

expedition members were affected.'

'And the fact we've got three other cases means that it wasn't the mere act of going into the crater which is important. So we have to discover why some people should have this apparent immunity and not others.' Carine sat forward, brows puckered in concentration. 'As far as I can tell, there's nothing that would explain it.'

'What about blood groups?'

'We checked that right away,' Corval said. 'Two of the men in the first expedition have the same blood group as the man who died.'

'Anything else in their medical history that might explain it?'

'Nothing.' Corval shrugged helplessly. 'I've been through their medical records thoroughly.'

Naysmith finished his coffee and set the cup down. 'We've also got to take its specificity into account, I suppose. I mean, the fact that it attacks only the optic nerve. Obviously it enters through the pupil since that is always — '

He froze for a second and in that

moment, the nagging, elusive thought that had been hiding at the back of his mind, popped into the open.

'I've been a goddamn, bloody fool!' he said tightly. 'It's been staring me in the face all this time and I completely missed it.' He thrust back his chair, almost knocking it over, and got quickly to his feet.

Corval stared up at him in surprise. 'Where are you going?'

'I've got to check Brander's records. I think I've got the answer to this whole damned problem.'

He knew the others were watching him curiously, probably thinking he had gone out of his mind, as he hurried out of the canteen. But he scarcely noticed this. His mind was too full of the stark realisation that had come to him, that he could think of nothing else.

9

At the bend in the corridor, Naysmith came to the temporary airlock. In his excitement he had forgotten they were completely cut off from the rest of the base.

He hesitated and then punched the button. Nothing happened. The door remained closed.

Damn, he thought viciously, this would happen. Now just how was he to communicate with Brander.

A voice broke in on his thoughts coming from the small communicator over the door, which he noticed for the first time. It was a voice he didn't recognise.

'Who's there?' it called.

'Doctor Naysmith. Open up. This is important.'

'I'm sorry, doctor.' Evidently the other was one of the security men. 'My orders are no one is to come out until Major Brander says so.'

'Then for Christ's sake get Brander.'

'I don't know if I — '

'Listen,' Naysmith forced patience into his voice. 'Switch Brander to this communicator. Tell him who I am and it's urgent.'

'All right. I'll try.'

There was a pause while Naysmith fretted impatiently. Then Brander's voice came on. 'Is that you, Naysmith? I've been trying to get you for the last ten minutes. We've got another four cases of this disease. I've alerted Schwartzwald and I want Doctor Corval here on the double. I've got no other choice but to put Directive Sterilisation AB-6 into operation.'

Naysmith stiffened. He said quickly. 'You gave us seventy-two hours, remember. That isn't up yet and — '

'I'm sorry. But circumstances have changed drastically. I can't take the risk of waiting any longer.'

'For God's sake, just listen to me for a minute.' Naysmith suddenly realised he was shouting. 'We've got the serum. There's every chance it will work. Two of those patients have already been injected

215

with it. But there's something else. I think I know now why only certain people are attacked by the virus and if I'm right we can check this disease without too much trouble. But I've got to go through your records.'

During the ensuing pause, Naysmith realised that his heartbeat had speeded up and he felt chill in every limb.

'To check those records means you'll have to come up to my office.'

'If you're worried about me spreading this disease, or catching it yourself, put it out of your mind. As far as I can tell, I'm not even carrying the disease.'

'How can you be certain of that?'

'Why the hell do you think I want to see those records?'

Naysmith felt his exasperation get the better of him. 'Now are you going to let me see them or not?'

'All right. Come on up. If you're wrong it won't make any difference, I suppose.'

So you've already committed yourself to blowing up the entire base, Naysmith thought dully as the airlock door slid open and he walked through. God, I hope

I'm right and I can convince him there's no need to wipe out all these people.

The man on the other side of the airlock was a soldier with a stun rifle over one shoulder. He gave Naysmith an almost frightened look as he stepped hastily out of the way.

Brander was alone in his office when Naysmith entered without knocking. There was no mistaking the deep lines of strain etched into the other's almost skeletal features.

'I want to see the file records of all those men who went on the two expeditions to Lowell,' he said quickly.

For a moment, the other eyed him curiously. He said nothing.

'I presume you have them here.'

'Who . . . oh, yes.' He got to his feet and went to the console in the corner. 'They're all stored in the computer. But I don't see what they can tell you.'

Naysmith waited impatiently while the security chief used the computer, feeling the tension begin to mount in him.

'This will only take a few seconds. Then we'll have a printout.'

The information came chugging through on the printer. It dropped a sheet of paper into a tray. Snatching it up, Brander held it out to him, watching him closely.

Naysmith scanned it rapidly, picking out the items that were of interest to him.

```
PERSONNEL RECORDS
SELECTED PERSONS CODE SB/662/X.40
ROBERTS ARTHUR    MALE  HEIGHT  5 FT  8 IN
                  WEIGHT 181 LB
                  HAIR BROWN EYES BROWN
                  DISTINGUISHING MARKS 0
                  FILE 616/CZ
THORPE SIMON      MALE  HEIGHT  6 FT  0 IN
                  WEIGHT 222 LB
                  HAIR BROWN EYES HAZEL
                  DISTINGUISHING MARKS 0
                  FILE 599/CX
MORELL PETER      MALE  HEIGHT  5 FT  6 IN
                  WEIGHT 178 LB
                  HAIR BLOND EYES BLUE
                  DISTINGUISHING MARKS 0
                  FILE 622/CX
POLOWSKI JAN      MALE  HEIGHT  6 FT  1 IN
                  WEIGHT 186 LB
                  HAIR BROWN EYES BROWN
```

	DISTINGUISHING MARKS 0
	FILE 602/CZ
MASON ARNOLD	MALE HEIGHT 5 FT 9 IN
	WEIGHT 216 LB
	HAIR BLACK EYES BROWN
	DISTINGUISHING MARKS 0
	FILE 609/CX
GORDOM ALAN	MALE HEIGHT 5 FT 7 IN
	WEIGHT 170 LB
	HAIR BROWN EYES BLUE
	DISTINGUISHING MARKS 0
	FILE 605/CX
KORDER FRANZ	MALE HEIGHT 5 FT 6 IN
	WEIGHT 155 LB
	HAIR BLACK EYES BROWN
	DISTINGUISHING MARKS 0
	FILE 586/CZ
DARVEL JOHN	MALE HEIGHT 6 FT 1 IN
	WEIGHT 202 LB
	HAIR BLOND EYES BROWN
	DISTINGUISHING MARKS 0
	FILE 607/CZ

'Well?' Brander asked tensely.

'It all fits. Hell, we should have thought of it before. That's the answer.'

'What is?' The security chief stared

down at the sheet, perplexed.

'The one feature about those two men who died that isn't shared by any of the others. The organism only attacks those with blue eyes. The others are unaffected.'

'But why? Surely there must be some explanation.'

'There is. Look at it this way. At birth, every baby is born with blue eyes. Many retain these for the rest of their lives. But others, those with brown or hazel eyes have a second layer, which forms shortly after birth. It all has to do with genetics but my guess is something in this additional film, almost certainly the pigment, prevents entry of the virus,'

'So those men we have in quarantine right now are harmless?'

'I doubt if they're even harbouring the virus now. These organisms usually die off extremely rapidly if they can't attack the host. It's one of the inherent weaknesses they have.'

'So we quarantine all personnel on the base with blue eyes until we're certain they aren't affected, then ship them out.'

'The answer may not be as drastic as

that. Quarantine them, of course. But first drop that thermonuclear device on Lowell. Once that's done and we've destroyed the source, this thing will burn itself out. If Corval's serum works, it should be possible to prevent any further spread throughout the base.'

'I'll get onto it right away.' The security chief's lips curved slightly and Naysmith realised it was the first time he had seen the other smile.

★ ★ ★

'It was so simple we were almost certain to overlook it,' Naysmith said, much later. 'I was so engrossed looking for other factors that I failed to see it.'

'That bomb was dropped half an hour ago, by the way,' Corval said. 'It completely obliterated Lowell. There'll be some residual radioactivity there for a time and unfortunately it destroyed all the evidence for the formation of that crater.'

'It was a small price to pay. We can only hope there isn't another region like that waiting to burst through the surface, some place where another meteorite lies buried.'

Carine said quietly, 'I wonder where it came from originally? The meteorite, I mean.'

Much of Naysmith's initial elation had gone now but he still felt some of the intense excitement overlying the inevitable relaxation of mind and body. 'It could have come from anywhere out there.' He gestured towards the early morning sunlight. 'It may not even have come from within our solar system. Space is so vast and there must be millions of other planetary systems circling other suns. It could have come from any one of them.'

Corval nodded. 'I reckon our friend Freeman may be able to give some answers to that. At least, it provides him with one fact he never had before. We can no longer regard ourselves as the only group of life forms in the galaxy.'

'And what about the position in the base?' Carine asked, looking at Corval.

The other smiled faintly. 'We seem to

have things under control here. The two patients I injected have responded to the treatment with the serum. No sign of any side-effects apart from some pronounced drowsiness.'

'Have those politicians circling around in orbit been told?'

'Brander told them a little while ago. Apparently, they've changed their mind about landing here. By now, they'll be on their way back to Earth.'

'With full and lurid details of all that happened, no doubt.'

'I guess so.' Corval leaned back and stared up at the ceiling for a moment. 'So they were the Martians, eh? Who'd have thought it.'

He sat silent for a long moment, then lowered his gaze, resting it on Naysmith.

'What do you intend doing now? They got you here under false pretences. There doesn't seem much for you to do now. You've met what was presumably the only so-called indigenous species on Mars and if Lowell was the only place they existed, the rest of the planet must be completely sterile.'

Naysmith thought for several seconds before answering. Then he said softly: 'The first thing I intend to do is sleep the clock around. Then I'd like to take a long, leisurely look around the base, possibly take a few more trips out into the deserts. That is, if I can find anyone who'll take on the job of acting as guide.'

He glanced directly at Carine as he spoke.

The girl's lips curved into a warm, understanding smile. 'I'd be glad to show you around, John.'

Somehow, he had the impression that the smile and the look in her eyes held the promise of something more and for the first time since landing on Mars, he felt at ease within himself.

THE END

We do hope that you have enjoyed reading this large print book.

Did you know that all of our titles are available for purchase?

We publish a wide range of high quality large print books including:
Romances, Mysteries, Classics
General Fiction
Non Fiction and Westerns

Special interest titles available in large print are:
The Little Oxford Dictionary
Music Book, Song Book
Hymn Book, Service Book

Also available from us courtesy of Oxford University Press:
Young Readers' Dictionary
(large print edition)
Young Readers' Thesaurus
(large print edition)

For further information or a free brochure, please contact us at:
Ulverscroft Large Print Books Ltd.,
The Green, Bradgate Road, Anstey,
Leicester, LE7 7FU, England.
Tel: (00 44) **0116 236 4325**
Fax: (00 44) **0116 234 0205**

F.B.I. SPECIAL AGENT

Gordon Landsborough

Cheyenne Charlie, Native American law student turned G-Man, is one of the Bureau's top agents. The New York office sends for him to investigate a sinister criminal gang called the Blond Boys. Their getaway cars somehow disappear in well-lit streets; they jam police radios; and now they've begun to add brutal murder to their daring robberies. Cheyenne follows a tangled trail that leads him to a desperate fight to the death in the beautiful scenery of the Catskill Mountains . . .